FRANKIE LOU'S BA

Create a church choir filled with teenage misfits?

Over Poppy's dead body.

Minister's daughter Frankie Lou McMasters has come back to Ruby Springs, Texas with her daughter, Betsy, eleven years after running off to marry the town bad boy. Her mild notoriety as a bad girl is prime gossip for her childhood enemy, Poppy Fremont, now choir director of Faith Community Church—where Frankie Lou's daddy, now retired to Florida, was the preacher.

When Frankie Lou comes to the deacons with a request to add a youth choir of at-risk teens she's been coaching, Poppy throws a fit. A few hours later, Frankie Lou finds her dead in the baptistery pool. And Poppy's not playing possum.

Frankie Lou sets out to clear her name as the main suspect, and tries to locate the real killer. Could he be sexy Joe Camps, the father of one of her teen singers? In the meantime, her momma shows up from Florida to take charge of Frankie Lou's life. Bless her heart.

Bringing in the Thieves

by

Lora Lee

Bell Bridge Books

This is a work of fiction. Names, characters, places and incidents are either the products of the author's imagination or are used fictitiously. Any resemblance to actual persons (living or dead), events or locations is entirely coincidental.

Bell Bridge Books
PO BOX 300921
Memphis, TN 38130
Print ISBN: 978-1-61194-465-5

Bell Bridge Books is an Imprint of BelleBooks, Inc.

Copyright © 2014 by Loralee Lillibridge writing as Lora Lee

Printed and bound in the United States of America.

All rights reserved. No part of this book may be reproduced in any form or by any electronic or mechanical means, including information storage and retrieval systems, without permission in writing from the publisher, except by a reviewer, who may quote brief passages in a review.

We at BelleBooks enjoy hearing from readers.
Visit our websites
BelleBooks.com
BellBridgeBooks.com
ImaJinnBooks.com

10 9 8 7 6 5 4 3 2 1

Cover design: Debra Dixon
Interior design: Hank Smith
Photo/Art credits:
Cover Art © Brian Rhedd

:Ltbn:01:

Acknowledgements

There are many to whom I owe sincere thanks for their part in getting this book published. The journey has taken me longer than I'd planned.

Laurie K., for always being the driver. You're the best travel buddy ever.

Nancy G., I'm a better writer because of you, my friend.

Florence P., my Girl Friday, for taking the worry out of the social media part of my life.

DebS and DD and the Bell Bridge Books staff, for your patience and understanding through the rough patches and making this book possible. I'm forever grateful.

Eileen D., for baseball, Ireland and oh, so many reasons.

My family, for your love and support.

And always, Gordie, for sixty years and counting. Remember the good times.

Chapter One

I knew the minute I read the church bulletin that I was fixin' to be Southern-fried and plated-up in front of God, the Faith Community Church deacons, and eventually the entire community of Ruby Springs, Texas, sure as my name's Frankie Lou Birmingham McMasters.

My well-meaning landlady, Nettie Bloom, had decided to announce my proposed church project without asking me if I wanted her to. I had just scheduled a meeting with the deacons about it, not given them any details about the idea. I hadn't spoken it aloud to anyone but Miss Nettie. But now there it was in print, along with Miss Nettie's usual assortment of misplaced phrases and Mrs. Malaprop word choices. Miss Nettie had been editing the church's newsletter, News From The Pews, for a good many years, but I'd noticed her memory getting a little tangled lately.

NEWS FROM THE PEWS

FAITH COMMUNITY CHURCH
100 Blessings St.
Ruby Springs, Texas

As we wait for the selection of a full-time pastor, we welcome back interim minister, Reverend Matthew Whitlaw to the pulpit next Sunday at Faith Community. His morning sermon will be "Jesus Walks on Water" followed by "Searching for Jesus" in the evening.

For those of you who have children and don't know it, we have a nursery downstairs.

Members of the Weight Watchers group will meet Monday at 5:30 P.M. for weekly weigh-in. Please use large double door at the side entrance to the annex. The Low Self-Esteem Support Group will be using the back door.

Prior to prayer meeting Wednesday evening, a bean supper will be held in the church hall. Special music will follow.

Until further notice, please give massages to the church secretary, Lovey Muchmore. She will then give massages to the newsletter editor who will share the details in our newsletter.

SPECIAL ANNOUNCEMENT: A NEW CHOIR FOR TEEN SINNERS IS BEING FORMED AND WILL COMPETE IN THE SLUMBER FUN AT THE CITY PARK NEXT MONTH. For more information on sinning contact Frankie Lou McMasters at Doc Adderly's Animal Clinic.

Prayerfully submitted,
N. Bloom, Newsletter Editor

Truth be known, there were certain people who weren't exactly thrilled by my return to the town where my daddy, Reverend Frank Birmingham, occupied the pulpit at Faith Community before his recent retirement to Florida. I'd been gone from Ruby Springs eleven years, but it seems those certain people have the combined memory of a herd of elephants. One in particular: Poppy Rose deHaven Fremont, Faith Community's choir director.

I grabbed my tote, made a quick call next door to Miss Nettie's house, where my eleven-year-old, Betsy, was staying for dinner, then headed for the church. It was a hot spring night and bound to get hotter.

Help me, Lord, Miss Nettie and that newsletter are gonna get me killed one way or another.

THE UNEXPECTED appearance of Poppy Rose deHaven Fremont in the church's conference room confirmed what I'd feared all along. My notoriety as the shamefully irreverent preacher's daughter hadn't been forgotten, even after an absence of more than a decade. Any hope of getting the deacons to approve my request had just been deep-sixed. Well, horse pucky!

There she was, the undisputed Queen of Mean, flapping her collagen-plumped lips faster than a whippoorwill's tail in a windstorm while seven deacons stared in wide-eyed amazement.

I shook my head in disbelief. What in the heck had she done to herself? Those puffy lips weren't the only recently enhanced body parts, either. Poppy Rose was a walking, talking endorsement for the modern wonders of plastic surgery and extreme weight loss. My monthly house rent couldn't begin to touch the high-dollar cost of that hot pink linen skirt and knit top clinging to her man-made curves closer than a coat of paint from Howard's Hardware. Talk about extreme makeover, her body had been nipped and tucked in places I didn't even want to think about. Yikes!

A brief but uncomfortable sting of envy zapped me so hard I could almost hear my momma saying, "Pretty is as pretty does, Frances Louise." A die-hard fan of *Downton Abbey*, she never called me Frankie Lou when she was in her Lady Louisa mood.

Poppy Rose teetered toward me on nose-bleed-high stilettos, her over-enhanced boobs leading the way. *Oh boy, here it comes,* I thought, wondering if escape was possible. Had she seen the bulletin?

"Well, Ah declare, Frankie Lou." Her words dripped so much toxic sweetness it made my teeth ache. "Here y'all are, stirring up trouble just like old times. You haven't changed a bit, bless your heart." She smiled, the bright flash of Hollywood-white teeth threatening to blind me on the spot.

I flicked a wayward strand of my straight black hair behind one ear. Now, truth is I don't give a horse's *patoot* about fashion, but does Starbucks know she's got her Texas-big hair whipped up like a mocha latte with caramel swirls?

"Why, hello, Poppy Rose," I said, sucking in my tummy and sticking out my 34B girls like they were double Ds. Hey, I have my pride, but there's no way I would ever let anyone slice and dice my body for the sake of "perfect."

According to Miss Nettie, Poppy Rose married into big money three years ago after meeting her future husband on a singles cruise. Miz Parvis Fremont turned her brand-new wealth into a mighty fine shopping career.

The impressive Fremont mansion and its extravagant interior adornments is the town's only claim to fame. Miss Nettie said Poppy Rose consulted a designer from Italy for the elaborate decorating, and the place got written up in some big architectural magazine. That bit of information teased my curiosity, but I'm not likely to ever be invited to the Ruby Springs' wonder home. In the first place, I wasn't even invited to the nuptials. Wouldn't have attended anyway, since the ceremony took place during my prolonged self-exile in Austin. I understand that show-of-the-century-shindig cost a cool half-million dollars, all paid for by the groom, of course. There was even actual dancing at the reception over at the town community center, something never done before in Ruby Springs. Yes indeedy, Poppy Rose finally snagged herself a wealthy spouse. Kind of sad he died so soon. Or was it? Looking at her now, I'd say she wears her hot pink widow's weeds just a little too perky.

A quick scan of Poppy Rose's high-fashion apparel made me wish I'd done a better job of making my appearance more polished and professional-looking this evening. Unfortunately, raising a twelve-year-old daughter and working at Doc Adderly's animal clinic every day barely gives me time for basic personal grooming, let alone extras like makeup and hair styling. Right or wrong, what you see is what you get, to quote an overused cliché.

I knew Parvis Fremont's untimely death last year had shocked the community because his demise had been the main topic of gossip at my first coffee klatch with Miss Nettie after I'd moved in next door to her four weeks ago. According to her, Mr. Money Bags Fremont was in good health when he married his much younger bride, in spite of his advanced years. Everyone accepted the cause of his death as age-related. However, Miss Nettie had her own opinion about the coroner's findings. In fact, she had opinions about a lot of happenings in Ruby Springs. She reads a lot of mystery and suspense novels.

She went on to relate how Poppy Rose, all decked out in widow's weeds and dripping with diamonds, had carried on hysterically at her husband's funeral, then left town the very next day for Dallas and a whirlwind shopping spree at Neiman Marcus.

Even though Poppy Rose held the highly-respected position of choir director at Faith Community now, I still couldn't wrap my mind around the possibility that she'd turned into a nice person after all these years. I mean, that would be a stretch of imagination for anyone who knew her.

Up until now, I hadn't told anyone about my meeting with the deacons tonight except Miss Nettie. The senior deacon, Mr. Botts, had assured me the agenda wouldn't be revealed until the men were all gathered at the church. I wondered if Poppy Rose had found out about it. But no matter if she knew, if she thought she could stop me from asking for the deacon's help, she was dead wrong, since Miss Nettie had jumped the gun. My bank account may not be as hefty as those belonging to the Rich and Rude Club of Ruby Springs, but I've got a sizable amount of good ol' Texas stubborn saved up that I haven't even used yet, so Miz Poppy Rose deHaven Fremont better watch her step. Just sayin'.

"Why, Poppy, you haven't changed either," I said in my best Southern-sweetness voice. "I knew you were the church music director, but when did you become a deacon? Or should I call you deaconess now?"

My question stopped her in her tracks. She puffed up like a balloon full of hot air, and I was wishing for a pin. Far as I was concerned, fawning over her new appearance wasn't happening, so if she expected flattery she'd have to look somewhere else.

Momma always said lying would get me "There" same as stealing, and I wasn't about to test the truth of her words. I knew where "There" was. Gaining back the respect of my hometown wasn't turning out to be as easy as I'd hoped, after all.

Before Poppy could sputter another sugary insult my way, Linwood Botts broke away from the knot of men and hurried toward me, all angles, long legs, and shiny-clean cowboy boots. With a lopsided half-smile obviously inhibited by nervousness, the lanky chairman of the deacons' board extended his hand like a true Texas rancher and gentleman.

"Good to see you, Frankie Lou. The deacons and I are eager to hear about the new project you mentioned in your phone call. But first, please join us for a glass of sweet tea before we get started. Emma Jean sent over some of her lemon bars, and there's plenty more desserts on the table. Go ahead on and help yourself to whatever strikes your fancy."

I thanked him and shook his hand, trying not to drool as I eyed the goodies. Deacon Botts's wife baked the best lemon bars that ever melted in my mouth. I left Poppy Rose standing there with her mouth agape and took off for the treats. *She hasn't seen the bulletin yet*, I thought. *Thank the Lord.*

The dessert table at the end of the otherwise austere conference room was a visual delight that brought back many childhood memories of church suppers and holiday celebrations.

Mint sprigs and lemon slices were artfully arranged on dainty serving dishes beside two delicate silver trays holding an assortment of scrumptious, homemade sweets. I recognized the tall, cut-glass pitchers chock-full of ice and sweet tea. Momma used to borrow them when she entertained the women's monthly Bible studies at the parsonage. The talented ladies of Faith Community had certainly outdone themselves with their culinary skills tonight.

Without giving a thought to calories, I picked up a dessert plate, put two of Emma Jean's delicious-looking lemon squares on it, and helped myself to a glass of cold, sweet tea. Since Betsy was eating at Miss Nettie's this evening, I'd skipped my own supper in order not to be late to the meeting. Carbs and sugar, yummy! My sweet tooth loved me, but my waistline hollered *HELP* on a daily basis.

Dessert-laden plate in hand, I turned around to look for a place to sit, and *WHAM!* I body-slammed right into You Know Who standing behind me closer than my own shadow.

The next few seconds were right out of a classic Three Stooges scene. Before you could say *pass the grits*, my plate turned into an airborne launching pad, and my sweet tea, lemon bars, and cupcake went flying.

One of the lemon bars morphed into a heat-seeking missile, burrowing deep inside the front of Poppy's knit top to settle who knows where. An ice cube followed the lemon bar down the path to Glory, sending good ol' Poppy into shock. She yelped and shimmied like a hip-gyrating Twenties' flapper. Good thing there wasn't a pole anywhere near her, or we'd all be praying for deliverance from evil. Behind me, seven bug-eyed deacons let out a collective murmur that sounded an awful lot like *Thank you, Jesus!*

Where my cupcake landed was anybody's guess, but my sweet tea baptized the rest of Poppy's expensive outfit without even so much as a *Hallelujah, Amen*! The stunned look on her perfectly made-up face was priceless. Just to be on the safe side, I said a prayer for help under my breath. I figured it couldn't hurt.

"Frankie Lou, you clumsy . . ." Poppy's face was redder than a ripe tomato from Miss Nettie's backyard garden.

Wilbur Hadley, one of the older deacons, rushed to the sputtering, jiggling woman's side with a handful of paper napkins and started dabbing at the front of her wet shirt.

When he wandered a little too close to her No Trespassing area, she slapped his hands and let out another nails-on-a-chalkboard screech. "Stop that, Wilbur, you idiot!"

Startled, the poor man backed away from the hysterical woman so fast he stumbled over his own feet and landed smack on his striped seersucker-clad keester. His fluttering hands flew up, and napkins scattered everywhere in a white paper blizzard. He tried to speak but couldn't. His Adam's apple bobbed up and down so hard it knocked his lime green bowtie crooked.

Linwood Botts hurried over to help the distraught Wilbur back to his seat and fetched him a glass of water.

It was impossible not to laugh. I clapped a hand over my mouth to stifle my chuckle. Couldn't help it. Mr. Botts, with his wild shock of gray hair, resembled a tall and wiry Ichabod Crane. Bald-pated, short-statured Deacon Hadley reminded me of one of those painted ceramic garden gnomes that lurked in Miss Nettie's flower beds. All he needed was a beard, a pointed hat, and green pants, but he'd have to ditch the bow tie.

The other five deacons were still staring but not at Wilbur. Oh no, their gazes were fastened on Poppy Rose, who could've won First Place in a wet tee-shirt contest with her expensive knit top shrunk up tighter than a two dollar bargain. As far as the men were concerned, wet was all that counted.

Shamefully, I enjoyed her moment of discomfort. While I retrieved the scattered napkins from the floor, I sincerely hoped poor Wilbur's excitable bachelor heart didn't go into shock from Poppy's Oscar-worthy hysteria.

"Here, Poppy, let me," I said, napkins poised to take up where Wilbur left off. "After all, this is my fault for not realizing you were in such a hurry to get to the desserts."

Faster than lightning, she zapped me with a stink eye and snatched the napkins right out of my hands.

"Oh, give those to me!" Pressing them against her baptized bosom, she leaned right in my face and whispered, "And if you don't drop your crazy plans for that choir right now, Frankie Lou, I promise you'll regret ever coming back to Ruby Springs."

Her last threat sizzled in my ear. So she *did* know!

Old resentment reared its ugly head, and it was all I could do to keep from smacking her upside her nipped-and-tucked face. I squeezed the wad of leftover napkins in my hand instead. That woman was more irritating than beach sand in my bikini.

Thankfully, she whirled off for the ladies room in a wet, lemon-scented huff, saving me the disgrace of committing a major No- No.

The deep-breathing I did to calm myself didn't work worth a hoot, only made my stomach growl. I needed nourishment. What I didn't need was Poppy Rose dragging my past through the muck of local gossip again. There had to be a way to stop her without getting arrested.

After Miss Bump-and-Grind stomped off to the ladies room for re-pairs, two of the deacons dragged mops and buckets from the storage closet, and everyone got to work doing cleanup. Everyone except me, that is. I wanted to help, but the men unanimously refused my offer, making me wonder if No was fixin' to be their operative word the rest of the evening. Talk about starting off on the wrong foot.

Since there was nothing more for me to do but wait until order was restored, I took advantage of Poppy's absence and indulged in two more lip-smacking lemon bars from the goody table, washing them down with a fresh glass of sweet tea. My nervous system welcomed the much-needed surge of sugar-loaded energy with a groan of pure pleasure. I enjoyed the momentary high as I mentally whizzed through the notes I'd prepared, frantically reworking my speech. While waiting for her return, I pulled my trusty notebook from my tote and scribbled down the changes before I forgot them. Poppy may have botched up the evening so far, but I wasn't going down without a fight. I needed the deacons on my side, and by gosh, I intended to have them before I left tonight.

Fifteen minutes later the men had finished their cleanup and were seated behind the long table again, backin' and forthin' with their heads together like men are inclined to do. Those same heads swiveled like a bunch of hoot owls when a dried-out and slightly disheveled Poppy Rose charged back into the room like Custer at Little Big Horn, her bejeweled hands flashing brighter than the bubble gum lights on a cop car.

"You won't get away with this, Frankie Lou McMasters!" Her screech endangered eardrums everywhere.

"Get away with what? Lord love a duck, Poppy Rose. You were standing behind me closer than white on rice. I already said I was sorry. It was an accident."

I eyed Poppy's pathetic attempt at damage control and grimaced. Talk about a repair job gone bad. The restroom's outdated automatic hand dryer must've blown itself right off the wall. New wrinkles were dried in places where there'd been none BBBT—Before Baptism By Tea. Even a non-fashionista like me could see the knit top was ruined. The future of that linen skirt looked pretty iffy, too. Both pieces were now two sizes smaller.

Doing some quick mental math, I roughly estimated the cost of replacing the two items versus the balance in my checkbook and swallowed a groan. Not even close. Then, without the teensiest bit of guilt, I deep-sixed any notion of reimbursing her for damages and threw up my hands in frustration. With all her money, she could afford new clothes any time. I could barely afford rent and groceries.

"I'm not talking about your boorish clumsiness, Frankie Lou. I'm talking about this!" She waved a piece of paper in my face as she passed, then slammed the thing down on the table in front of the deacons and leaned over in Earl Moss's face so close his eyes nearly popped out of his head. "Just take a look right here!"

Believe me, Earl looked, all right, and so did the other deacons, but not at any piece of paper. Not with her bosom stuck right out there like twin torpedoes. Earl nearly choked on his sweet tea, and I swear Wilbur Hadley squealed under his breath.

"Have y'all read this?" Poppy's screech-owl demand was just shy of glass-shattering pitch. "I'm telling y'all, the church simply cannot allow this fiasco to happen. Frankie Lou should be banned from evah being in charge of any church functions. Evah, y'all hear?"

Evah? "Now wait just a darn minute, Poppy Rose," I said. All of a sudden my blood pressure started shooting for the high numbers. Who did she think she was? My fists were balled so tight if I'd had fancy, glued-on fingernails like Poppy's my palms would be shredded. "You should get the facts before you go spouting stuff like that." My head pounded with the stress of trying not to yell back. Calm was *not* how I was feeling.

"Oh, I've got facts," she said, her face getting redder by the minute, "right here." She stabbed the paper with a hot pink fingernail. "You've gone behind our backs and started a new singing group with a bunch of street punks! It says so right here in the church newsletter. A choir for sinners!"

Her outburst of hot air blew Earl's toupee slightly off center. Wild-eyed, he scrambled to grab it and scooted his chair back out of her way like he was afraid she might jump over the table. A definite probability in her overblown exasperation, however, she kept right on ranting and waving her hands.

"Do y'all know what will happen if you let *those* kind of hoodlums into the church? Well, I'll tell you. They'll be carrying on like a bunch of heathens, that's what. And, that's not all." The drama queen executed a long, theatrical pause before she continued. The deacons froze in their seats like deer caught in headlights. "The church's name will be smeared all *ovah* the county. Shameful, that's what it'll be. Downright shameful. I insist you put a stop to this right now. Y'all hear me?" She rolled her eyes heavenward. "Lord, have mercy on us all."

Now, Poppy Rose was full of a lot of things when we were in school, but religion definitely hadn't been one of them. However, the deluxe hissie-fit-with-a-tail-on-it she was pitching on behalf of the church right now earned a five-star rating, bless her heart. Nothing would make her happier than to see me barred from Faith Community membership forever, but hey, I wasn't about to let that happen. Not now, not ever.

Poppy read aloud. "New choir for teen sinners being formed to compete in the slumber fun next month. For more information on sinning contact Frankie Lou McMasters *at Doc Adderly's Animal Clinic.*"

"That should be *SINGERS*, not sinners", I yelled over the rising male chatter. "It's a youth choral group, for cryin' out loud, and *SUMMER FEST*, not a slumber party!"

No one heard me, of course. How could they? They were all talking at once, noisier than a flock of angry blue jays sitting on a hot wire. I didn't even try to explain that I wasn't a contact for information on sinning. Lawd!

Poppy Rose kept on yammering and waving the bulletin at the deacons huddled together like Faith Community's version of the United Nations settling a world conflict. Bless her devious heart.

I'm not a preacher's kid for nothing. I can *Hallelujah* with the best of 'em, and I intended to do just that.

Chapter Two

Naturally, being the choir director and all, Poppy was dead set against anything that threatened her lofty position in the church. It's my guess she assumed I hadn't changed since Daddy and his shotgun convinced good-looking, sweet-talking Billy John McMasters that marrying me was the smart thing to do. Huh! Who knew Daddy owned a shotgun?

Back then, everyone in town knew about Poppy's not-so-secret crush on sexy B.J. Thanks to Poppy Rose and her gossipy circle of followers, my reputation as *hard-to-handle* changed to *disgraceful* as quick as my wedding. The only contact I've had with Billy John since our split is when his meager child support check arrives every month. Unfortunately, B.J.'s good looks and sexy smile had blinded me to the truth about his tomcattin' personality. He'd also been an expert at eyeballing every woman from sixteen to sixty, the cheating jerk. When the divorce became final I vowed never to ride that love train again. No way! I've learned about life the hard way since then, and I'm a smarter person for it, but Poppy Rose still behaved like a witch's apprentice, stirring the gossip cauldron with her vindictive stick just to make me look bad.

I had hoped my past behavior would be considered water under the Ruby Springs Bridge by now, but no such luck. Like it or not, Poppy was determined to dam up all that murky water caused by my youthful mistakes and drag my tarnished reputation through it again for another round of damaging untruths. I declare, the woman's worse than that drum-beating pink bunny. She never stops.

While I waited for the deacons' reaction to Poppy Rose's fuss, uneasiness cat-pawed its way down my spine. Would my scandalous past sway their decision and result in a NO vote? The few weeks I've been back in town haven't been long enough to determine which way the stream of gossip flowed. The deacons' frowns had me wondering if Judgment Day was coming a little too soon.

Linwood Botts rose and motioned me forward as he addressed the assembled group. "Let me remind you, gentlemen, our duty as responsible deacons is to put the church's welfare first. We must also be charitable toward the individual needs of our members. Frankie Lou will be allowed to speak."

As if their mommas had suddenly given them a group thump on their noggins to remind them of their manners, the men groaned in unison and slowly shuffled to their feet.

Mr. Botts held up a restraining hand. "You may remain seated, gentlemen, but please be courteous and give Frankie Lou your undivided attention."

Given the age of the majority of the deacons, their collective sigh of relief as they settled back in their seats made me chuckle under my breath.

The senior deacon directed his next words toward the disheveled Poppy Rose. "Feel free to leave any time, Miz Fremont. You're not obliged to stay."

Naturally, Poppy didn't budge an inch, just stood there with her mouth all puckered up funny like she'd been sucking lemons all day. I ignored her and conveyed my thanks to the deacons with a smile as I passed each of them a printout of my proposal.

When I'd set up this meeting during an earlier phone conversation, Mr. Botts informed me the interim pastor, Reverend Whitlaw, was out of town and wouldn't be at the meeting. Since Doc was nice enough to let me use the computer and printer at the clinic, I only printed out enough copies for the seven board members. After all, I didn't want to push my employer's generosity too far by abusing the use of his paper and printer ink after he refused to let me pay for the expenses.

The apparent interest of the deacons encouraged me as I began my proposal. "Gentlemen, I appreciate your giving me this opportunity to—"

"Wait a minute, Frankie Lou. You forgot to give me a copy." Poppy interrupted with a wave of her hand, nearly knocking me over in her rush to speak.

For my own safety, I moved aside to give her more room. I swear that woman couldn't say a word if her hands were tied behind her back. I was tempted to do just that. Her whining grated on my already shaky nerves as much as her over-dramatic gestures.

"Sorry, Poppy Rose, but I only made enough for the deacons. If I'd known you were coming . . ." *I'd have baked a cake. Not!* The silly song lyrics popped into my head for no good reason, and now I had a darned earworm. Satan was trying his best to sabotage my efforts.

Poppy Rose shot a nasty scowl my way and stepped right smack in front of me, barely missing my foot.

"In that case, I have an extremely urgent matter to discuss with the deacons first." Slowly, she studied each of the men seated in front of her. "There's absolutely no reason for Faith Community to sponsor another entry in the Summer Fest. That's a blatant conflict of interest. Remember," her voice escalated to a higher pitch, wobbling on its way up, "the church choir won First Place in the competition last year under my direction. Frankie Lou's silly notion to enter her little group of amateurs is ridiculous. The church doesn't need two entries competing in the contest!" Her well-shaped eyebrows arched in a *y'all will nevah be in my league* sort of glare that sent blips of righteous indignation marching hand in hand with my pride.

When she stamped her foot like a pouting child hell-bent on getting her own way, determination burned through me like a shot of white lightning. (Don't ask how I know about that.) I was primed and ready to fight for my rights. Lesson number one from my side: never challenge a preacher's kid.

"Listen here, Poppy Rose, my group is not—"

Mr. Botts shot a warning glance my way and pressed one finger to his lips. Huh? I didn't like that at all, but I clamped my mouth shut, anyway. My thoughts, however, kept right on going.

The senior deacon turned to the sputtering choir director. "We're not saying you can't enter the choir in the competition this year, Poppy Rose. Frankie Lou's plan won't interfere with that in any way. Right, Frankie Lou?"

I nodded. "Of course, it won't. My group will be—"

Once again Mr. Botts cut me off with a quick shake of his head, making me wonder if I'd ever get the chance to deliver a complete a sentence here tonight.

"Frankie Lou's group is younger and more up-to-date. We hope it will encourage more youth to attend our church. Our attendance has fallen off greatly in the past few years," he reminded Poppy and the deacons. "I think you're all aware that our current membership consists mainly of retirees nowadays. Not that there's anything wrong with that," he added quickly. "Our senior members have plenty of experience to share, but unfortunately, there are very few young people willing to be mentored. Remember, we haven't even found anyone interested in filling our pulpit since our last pastor moved to another assignment two months ago. It's up to us to be fishers of men and begin casting our nets, so to speak. Frankie Lou's singing group is a perfect opportunity to bring more young people to the church and become influential mentors, as well."

Well, you'd have thought he'd slapped her the way Poppy Rose staggered back at the good deacon's words. With her hands pressed to her chest, she rolled her eyes in exaggerated shock. Oh, yeah, Drama Queen was back on stage and gearing up to pitch another hissie fit. Lucky us.

"What are you sayin', Linwood Botts? That I'm not up-to-date or a fishing-whatevah? Why, that's plain nonsense. I'm as updated as anybody in town." She stuck her nose in the air and got all huffy-like. "Frankie Lou's bunch of hoodlums are right off the streets. I've seen how they roam the neighborhood at night. Who knows what kind of trouble they'll make if we let them in here? Mark my words, deacons, they'll steal us blind. And another thing," she continued barely pausing to catch her breath. "Allowing a bunch of rowdy teenagers to represent our church will give the wrong impression of Faith Community's standards. Don't forget, y'all, I have final approval of any church activity that benefits from my late husband's very generous donations." She had the audacity to shake her finger at the row of men staring at her. "And . . . ," she lowered her voice to an ominous whisper, "Frankie Lou's reputation is not exactly spotless, either, if y'all know what I mean."

Okay, that bites. "I'm not asking for any financial help from the church funds," I insisted.

My hands curled into tight little fists to keep from popping her one in the mouth. I might be out of practice, but I'm pretty sure I could take her on with the skills I'd been forced to acquire in sixth grade.

"Poppy Rose, if you're referring to my actions years ago, that's your choice. But that's all in my past. God already knows I'm sorry. He and I are okay about that, not that it's any of your business. Now, could we please get on with the matter that brought us here tonight instead of regurgitating old gossip?"

One of the deacons I knew only by name stood up to speak. Brewster Carson appeared friendly enough. With his round belly and shock of white hair, he reminded me of Santa Claus without a beard.

"I think it's time we let Miz McMasters have her say like Deacon Botts said. We can open a discussion afterwards. Agreed?"

Deacon Carson's steel gray gaze issued a silent directive to the group of men. They nodded in agreement. All but one, that is. Norm Watkins was the exception. He scowled at me over the top of his wire-rimmed spectacles. What was up with that? I had no argument with him. In fact, the only time I'd had contact with him since I'd moved back to Ruby Springs was the time I stopped by his pharmacy to purchase ointment and bandages for Betsy's scraped knee. We exchanged a few words then, nothing more. His disapproving look this evening puzzled me.

I was still mulling over Watkins's odd manner when Deacon Carson turned and spoke quietly to Poppy. "Since this is supposed to be a closed board meeting, Miz Fremont, I must ask you to leave now."

For a long second, the only sound in the room was the collective gasps of the deacons. Poppy leveled a deadly glare at me, made a funny-sounding snarl, and fired one final, spite-fueled rocket.

"I promise you, Frankie Lou, the only way your gang of troublemakers can win the competition will be over my dead body."

With that, she stomped out of the room, slamming the door behind her hard enough to shatter windows.

Taking advantage of the calm after the Poppy storm, I mustered up my courage and proceeded to go after what I'd come for. "Gentlemen, thank you so much for taking time to listen to my plan. I hope you'll be as excited about the teen singers as I am, when you learn more about them."

AN HOUR LATER I had two good reasons for the smile on my face as I left the building. Reason number one was the approval for my singing group to use the church annex for rehearsals on Thursday nights. The second equally important reason was the plate of leftover lemon bars Mr. Botts had insisted on giving me. Mission accomplished with a sweet-tasting bonus.

As I left the church, a light rain drizzled through the humid evening to dampen my hair and make my clothes stickier than they already were. "Typical summer weather for Ruby Springs," I muttered to no one.

Bemoaning the fact that my aging minivan, nicknamed "Minnie," wasn't healthy enough to drive tonight, I dodged raindrops and hurried across to the tree-lined side of the street. Lately, my aging mode of transportation suffered from loud groans and coughing fits whenever I tried to start her. Unfortunately, saving enough money to replace my dinosaur-on-wheels with a newer model was as likely to happen as Santa's reindeer line-dancing in my front yard.

Fortunately, dreaming didn't cost anything.

Before my good sense had time to persuade me to change my mind, my feet took charge, and I found myself taking a slight detour on the way home. I covered the next few blocks in a dream-like fantasy of me behind the wheel of a super-van driving America's newest singing sensations, The Joyful Noise, to their next sold-out musical gig in style. How cool would that be? Lost in the totally absurd pipedream, I didn't even notice the drizzle had stopped until I saw the flashing, neon sign at the Best Deals on Wheels car lot.

Lordymercy, would you look at those beauties? Rows of shiny vans and luxury sedans were lined up across the paved lot like a box of rainbow-colored crayons. My hankering level shot to the moon and beyond so fast it sucked the breath right out of me.

Bold as a buyer with money to burn, I sashayed through the brightly-lit paths of temptation on my way to the back of the lot, wisely avoiding the brand new models. In the USED CARS section, jewel-like flags with messages of *Buy Me! Buy Me!* flew above the rows of gently-used beauties.

Good thing the dealership was closed and dreaming was free. Whoever was in charge of marketing at Best Deals on Wheels deserved an A+ for hooking me from the get-go. If my bank account had contained any balance at all, I might've succumbed to temptation and signed my name on an impossible contract for one of the nearly-new, full-sized vans on display.

I faced the fact that replacing my van someday was inevitable, and tonight I'd spotted the perfect model in the second row. Only two years old, the lipstick-red beauty with eight-passenger capacity was exactly what I'd dreamed about in my fantasy. I could almost see The Joyful Noise logo emblazoned on each side in neon colors. But replacing the van would involve money I didn't have right now. Besides, the group didn't have a logo yet, but hey, planning ahead was smart, right? And my plans for my young singers were beyond large. I could even see a grand tour bus in The Joyful Noise future someday. Why not?

Realistically, my wants were a long way from being met, so as a consolation prize I lifted the foil wrapping from the plate I was holding and downed one of the lemon bars.

When I finally pulled my attention away from the rows of four-wheeled enticements to check my watch, I couldn't believe it was nearly nine o'clock. I should've been home by now. Knowing Miss Nettie's tendency to fret, she was liable to have the cops out looking for me right this minute. Thank Heaven for modern technology and cell phones. I reached for my tote to get my phone only to realize the darn bag wasn't slung over my shoulder. I did a head slap. "Really, Frankie?"

How could I forget something as important as the tote I carried to work every day? The answer couldn't have been more obvious. Lemon bars and my silly fantasy dream about cars and singing gigs for The Joyful Noise had taken over my good sense. Now I had to figure a way out of my predicament. I knew darn well I couldn't afford anything on this car lot. I shouldn't even be here. When would I learn to control my "Oh, shiny!" moments?

I hot-footed back to the church, grumbling all the way. Could the day get any worse? For penance, I only allowed myself half of another lemon bar instead of the whole thing. The remaining two would have to wait until I got home.

Dusky pink twilight melted into deep purple as I hurried to retrace my steps. Street lights flickered like mischievous fireflies making shadows that played hide and seek in the darkened alleyways between the shops and office buildings.

Up and down Center Street the dim security lights glowing softly inside the local shops added a cozy charm to the little community, something I'd missed during my years in Austin. No big-name chain stores here in Ruby Springs. Not even a Walmart.

I veered off Center and wound my way back through the familiar neighborhoods of comfortable, middle-class homes with their wraparound Southern-style front porches. Stunning pink azaleas and fuchsia bougainvillea bloomed profusely, their beauty muted by the approaching darkness. Sadly, those lovely porches were empty. Technology had arrived in my sleepy hometown with a bang.

Along with the recent arrival of cable service to the area, more and more residents were abandoning their front porch rockers for family room recliners. Now, watching the latest news and entertainment in front of their new flat screen televisions replaced spending balmy, summer evenings outside gossiping with neighbors. The small community had been cautious about moving into the age of technology, but some of the changes were already in place before my return. In a way, I hated to see that slower-paced, friendlier lifestyle disappear.

Ethereal shadows played tag among the neatly-trimmed boxwood hedges along the building as I approached. Lights from within the church glowed through the stained glass windows.

I clearly remembered Mr. Botts making certain everything was taken care of before we all left the church. Maybe Elwood Hooper, the custodian, had come in early to clean for Sunday services. I paused on the sidewalk and scanned the back parking lot expecting to see his truck. The area was empty except for a single car parked beside a large industrial dumpster. A car that looked exactly like Poppy's.

Though Poppy Rose wasn't the only person in town who owned a Cadillac, she always parked away from the main area to avoid any nicks or scratches on her silver chariot. But since she'd stormed out of the meeting tonight well over an hour ahead of the rest of us, the car couldn't be hers.

Not my problem. My mood was too good to spoil wondering whether or not the vehicle was Poppy's. All I wanted was to grab my tote and get back home.

I cut across lawn and was halfway across the parking lot when the harsh glare of headlights bore down on me without warning. "Hey! Watch where you're going!" I yelled, stumbling to the side entrance in my dash for safety. The car I'd seen by the dumpster whizzed past close enough for me to glimpse a fuzzy pink pillow in the back window.

I picked myself up off the sidewalk and hurried to the street, but the sedan was out of sight. I hadn't been able to see the driver's face, but there was no doubt in my mind the car belonged to Poppy Rose. Miss Nettie'd caught me up on all the town gossip when I'd first moved into her rental next door. That's how I knew the pillow in that car was the one used in Poppy's wedding to carry the rings.

Rattled by the near miss and nursing a skinned knee, I limped the rest of the way into the church and down the hall to the annex. I entered the building humming *This Little Light of Mine*. I was determined to shine, one way or another.

Outside, the sinking sun's final rays painted the nearby houses with a gold-dipped artist's brush, but inside the conference room, the closed window curtains made it dark as the bottom of an empty well. The lights were off as I'd expected. I felt along the wall just inside the door, flipped the switch, and glanced around the room. All neat and tidy like I knew it would be. Nothing out of place except for my tote right on the chair where I'd left it.

With my free hand, I slipped the bag's strap over my shoulder, steadied the plate of lemon bars in my other hand, and turned off the light. I made my way back through the church, eager to get home to begin jotting down my ideas on paper.

The faint gurgle of running water caught my attention as I hurried past the pulpit. *If that's rain, I hope it's only a light shower.* There hadn't been any rain in the forecast, but what else could it be? Torn between curiosity to investigate the sound and my eagerness to get home and work on The Joyful Noise plans, I wasn't happy when my uninvited conscience butted in loud and clear.

Shame on you, Frankie Lou. You know that's not rain. What if a water pipe's broken somewhere and the sanctuary floods because you didn't take time to check it out? You want to be responsible for that?

"Oh, all right. Never argue with a stubborn conscience," I complained to the empty pews and headed back toward the raised dais to check out the baptistery. Never let it be said that Frankie Lou McMasters doesn't care enough about the church's welfare to do my duty as one of God's children. My personal wishes—and the lemon bars—would have to wait.

Even though the baptistery was hidden from view by heavy, wine-colored drapes, I knew the pool was never filled until right before a scheduled baptism. Every safety precaution was always observed. And baptismal services never took place after regular worship hours. An eerie shiver danced along my spine. *Hoo-boy, something's not right,* I thought.

I left my tote and the plate of goodies on one of the choir seats, pulled the drapes apart, and stuck my head in for a look.

"Oh, noooo!" A full stream of water poured from a wall faucet near the metal steps and splashed into the rising waters of the baptismal pool. Flood waters were inches from the top.

I raced through the tiny side room and into the inner chamber. I could've found the way with my eyes closed, but this time I kept them open, fearful that changes might have been made since my father had baptized me here when I was nine. In my rush to stop the flow of water, I realized I didn't know how to drain the pool. I'd have to call the maintenance man, but first I had to turn off the faucet

Haste really does make waste, I quickly learned. When I yanked a little too hard on the door to the baptistery, the handle came off in my hand and the door flew open. I staggered backwards, teetering precariously to keep my balance with my arms flailing like a crazy windmill, and completely missed the first metal step. My foot slid on the second, water-covered one, and next thing I knew, I was airborne like the rock out of David's sling-shot.

Before I could yell for help, my face slapped the water with a hard smack. The sting of the impact burned like fire on my cheeks. The rest of me made waves big enough for boogie-boarding. I shot up spitting water like a breaching whale and sloshed back toward the steps to give the faucet an angry twist. Whose inexcusable carelessness had caused this gosh-awful mess? I'd definitely be fixin' to report the matter soon as I could get to my phone. Why, who knows when the disaster would've been discovered if I hadn't come back for my tote? The entire church could've flooded by then.

I groaned and rubbed my stinging cheeks, bemoaning the condition of the dripping capris and shirt plastered to my body like I'd been paper maché'd with wet tissue paper. There was nothing to do now but stay soaked to the skin until I got home.

To add to the bizarre craziness of the evening, one of my sandals had launched in mid-flight when I hit the water and was somewhere on the bottom at the other end of the pool. Since buying new sandals wasn't in this month's budget, I was about to launch an underwater Search and Retrieve. Whoever left that faucet running owed me a new pair of shoes. Why was it turned on? I've never been a fan of water sports, certainly not in a baptistery, but I was not leaving without my shoe.

I shoved my stringy, wet hair out of my eyes, held my breath, and stuck my head under the water. Feeling like a mermaid in the supporting cast of *Finding Nemo*, I spotted the sandal not far from where I stood and reached for it. That's when my blurry underwater vision snagged on another much larger object. I sloshed over to investigate. I choked on my watery scream.

Lord have mercy!

Chapter Three

Trussed up like a Thanksgiving turkey, silver duct tape wrapped around her hands and ankles, Poppy Rose lay motionless on the bottom of the baptistery, her once-beautiful attire swaying gently with each ripple of the water. The hair so perfectly styled earlier floated out around her head like Medusa's snakes angry at being disturbed.

I burst out of the water, gulped another frantic breath of air and went back under. No time to be squeamish. I had to get Poppy Rose to safety and call for help.

Locking my arms around her waist, I dragged her water-soaked, inert body up the stairs and onto the narrow landing, gasping with every step. My clumsy efforts to free her hands failed. The duct tape binding her was the forever kind. Even if I'd known how to perform CPR, the way her arms were taped across her chest made it impossible. I screamed at her. I had to try, even though I feared the worst. "Poppy, can you hear me? Poppy Rose!"

Her head flopped back, eyes cloudy and sightless. *Oh no! Oh, God!* I felt for a pulse, but it was impossible to find one with the tape around her wrists. I pressed two fingers against the side of her neck. Nothing. Nada! Zip!

There has to be! Please God, there has to be! The desperate cry inside my head became a mantra. "Poppy!" I yelled over and over, even though I knew in my heart the effort was futile.

My cries echoed eerily back to me from the metal walls surrounding the baptistery. A wave of nausea swamped me so suddenly my stomach churned like buttermilk on its way to butter. I hung my head down until the queasiness passed, but my mind kept racing ahead of the sickly sensation. I had to get a grip and move. Poppy needed help now!

My wet, bare feet slapped across the floor as I bolted from the room. In my effort to rescue Poppy, both my sandals were now somewhere in the depths of the baptistery pool.

"Help! Somebody help!" I raced into the sanctuary with barely a breath left in my shaking body. Only the rush of adrenalin kept me from falling apart. My mind couldn't accept what I'd just seen. Someone evil beyond my imagination had left Poppy Rose to die. In the baptistery, of all places! Was that person still somewhere inside the church?

Terrified, I dug my phone out of my tote and with trembling, wet fingers dialed 9-1-1. Moments later three men wearing dark blue uniforms charged through the church's carved oak doors.

Wow! Talk about fast response. I rushed toward them. "Thanks guys. I'm so glad—"

"Hold it right there, lady," the tall, skinny one yelled. All three had me sighted in. I dropped the phone and shoved my hands in the air. Hey, I'm no dummy. I know better than to argue with cops brandishing guns.

BEFORE YOU COULD say "Lord love a duck," the bizarre scene inside the church turned into a bad crime movie with me smack in the middle of the action. One of the officers ushered me back into the sanctuary with polite orders to sit and wait to be questioned while another called the Emergency Unit. Soaking wet and shivering, I huddled in one of the pews and said a silent prayer for help.

The medics arrived and disappeared to work on Poppy Rose while the local crime scene squad, all six of them, swarmed over the place like an army of angry fire ants. I heard a big splash from the baptistery and wondered if the Ruby Springs law enforcement had called in scuba divers. Wouldn't letting the water drain out be a simpler solution?

The sergeant in charge of keeping an eye on me remained standing at the end of the pew. My guess was to prevent my escape. Horrified by what was happening, there was no way I'd risk skipping out before I had a chance to tell my side of the story. Confident the sooner I explained my part, the sooner I could go home, I resigned myself to waiting as long as it took. From their enthusiastic efforts, it was obvious the Ruby Springs PD was handling its first crime investigation.

Fifteen or twenty stressful minutes passed, giving me plenty of time to worry. Finally a bald, heavyset man with a reddish moustache appeared through the baptistery's side entrance. Dressed in brown slacks and a tan sport jacket over a wrinkled, dark blue knit shirt, he was frowning as he approached the pew and slid in beside me without so much as a *by your leave*. I scooted over to make room for his bulk.

"Detective Vince Hardy." He flipped open a small case, flashed his badge, and contemplated me through blue eyes cold enough to freeze ice cubes for a bathtub full of sweet tea.

"Frankie Lou McMasters," I countered, deciding manners were a lost art among the members of the Ruby Springs PD.

The detective put his badge away and pulled a small notebook and neon orange ballpoint pen from his jacket pocket. The fact that he began writing before I even told him anything rattled my water-logged composure enough to make me squirm. That and the fact I really had to pee.

"Well then, Miz McMasters," he said, looking up from his note-making, "the officers who answered the call reported you were the one who found the victim. I'd like to hear your version of what happened here tonight." He kept his pen poised and ready to write as if he expected me to have all the answers to tonight's mystery. *Huh! As if.*

Determined to cooperate, I described how I'd found Poppy Rose when I'd returned for my tote. "Anyone can see she's been murdered, Detective. Hog-tied in duct tape. A horribly gruesome way to die." Between shivers and sniffles, I told him everything I could remember, even admitting to the embarrassing accident earlier that evening in the conference room with Poppy and my dessert plate. He was bound to find out from the deacons, anyway. Besides, I had nothing to hide.

"So you and the victim had a fight before the meeting started?"

"No, of course not. I mean, not a real fight. I accidentally bumped into her when I turned around. My glass of iced tea spilled on her. Just an accident."

"And that's all that happened?"

I gulped. "Um, well, some of my dessert may have gotten on her clothes and messed them up a little, but no one was hurt. I mean, her clothes weren't totally trashed or anything. She cleaned up in the ladies room." He probably didn't give a flying fig about the fate of her designer outfit, but I told him anyway.

He kept writing. "And she left after that?"

"No, she stayed for part of the meeting."

"Hmmm. And the purpose of the meeting? Did it concern the deceased?"

"Not at all. I was there to ask the deacons for permission to use the church conference room for my choral group's rehearsals, that's all. Poppy wasn't involved in any part of it. I don't even know how she found out about it."

"So this was a secret meeting?"

Oh, for crying out loud! My defensive mode kicked in, and I jumped to my feet. "Detective, there was nothing secret about the meeting. It simply didn't involve anyone but the deacons and me. There was no public notice, if that's what you're getting at. We didn't take out an ad on television, either." I was getting a little steamed. His questioning was darn near accusatory. "Are we finished here, Detective?" I couldn't wait much longer to hit the ladies room down the hall.

"Please sit down, Miz McMasters. I assure you I'll only be a few minutes longer."

I sucked in my breath and gingerly sat down, my wet capris now uncomfortably stuck in a wedgie. Oh, great.

Oblivious of my squirming, Detective Hardy continued. "Is there anything else you can think of? Something you might have overlooked earlier? Anything at all?"

"No, nothing. I've told you everything I remember. Any of the deacons can verify what I've said."

He scribbled for a minute longer, looking up when he'd finished. "Oh, believe me, I'll be questioning everyone who was at the meeting, Miz McMasters. I'll obtain a list of all the deacons who attended."

I squeezed my hands together so tight my fingers were getting numb. The rest of me felt that way, too. I wondered aloud, not really expecting an answer. "Why would anyone want to kill Poppy Rose, Detective?"

"Good question, Miz McMasters, and the very reason we're here. Our job is to find out who and why. Rest assured we will find the guilty party sooner or later." His ice-blue eyes made contact with mine.

I shivered. The situation was beyond serious. It was catastrophic. Poppy Rose was dead, and I was the prime suspect. There was no witness to back up my spur-of-the-moment visit to the used car lot and over an hour of unaccounted-for time before I discovered Poppy and called for help. Proving my innocence did *not* look promising from where I sat. Not promising, at all.

"I'll do everything I can to cooperate, Detective Hardy," I assured him. Only false courage kept me from falling apart. "No matter what anyone says, I would never want something as horrible as this to happen to Poppy Rose or anyone."

Something in the way his eyebrows twitched told me he wasn't convinced. Before he could comment further, the medics wheeled the gurney down the aisle past us. Without asking permission, I rose and followed, sucking in a sob at the thought of Poppy Rose inside that body bag. Even though Poppy and I had had our differences, I never wished for her to die.

The minute we walked out the door I was startled by a flashbulb going off in my face. An eager reporter, hungry for information, pushed his way closer to where I stood with the detective, shouting questions as he advanced. Distraught, my bottled up emotions erupted in a flood of tears. Detective Hardy hurried me back inside the church, but not before the insistent reporter grabbed another shot of me being led away from the gurney by the detective's firm grip on my arm.

BACK INSIDE, THE detective informed me I would be taken downtown to headquarters by one of the sergeants to meet with the police chief. I wouldn't be allowed to go home and get out of my wet clothes, either. This whole ordeal was turning into a very long and unhappy night.

Detective Hardy paused briefly at the front of the sanctuary to have a few words with another member of the crime team. I was halfway to the choir room before he yelled at me and started running.

I yanked one of the purple choir robes from the row of garments hanging on a metal rack. I may not be the next Scarlett O'Hara in green drapes, but I wasn't about to meet the chief of police looking like I'd survived a shipwreck, either. On the way out, I passed a full-length mirror and moaned. My face was ashen, my dark eyes huge with shock. My hair hung limp and tangled. "Purple definitely isn't my color," I said, frowning at the image just as the red-faced detective arrived, huffing and puffing, to escort me back to the sanctuary. I hoped he'd received a clean bill of health at his last check-up. The way he was breathing, I didn't want him to stroke out.

"Miz McMasters," he said, when he'd managed to catch his breath, "don't you know running from the authorities will get you in trouble?"

"I only wanted to find something to wear over my wet clothes. Far as I know, that's no crime. I'll return the choir robe tomorrow. If I had wanted to run away from you, Detective, I would never have come back inside the church." I glared at him and pulled the voluminous folds tighter around me, thinking I must've grabbed one of the men's larger sizes.

"That may be," he said, taking my arm and ushering me back into the sanctuary, "but appearances can be deceiving. If you're smart, you won't invite more trouble than necessary."

A SHORT TIME later, his words of caution were still ringing in my ears as I climbed into the back seat of one of Ruby Springs's police cars.

Now, I'm almost thirty years old, but truth is, I've never been hauled off to any police headquarters until tonight. My very first ride in a squad car might've been exciting if I'd needed the research to write an article on the county's crime-fighting system. Unfortunately, that wasn't even remotely close to the reason why I was being driven downtown by two serious-looking RSPD officers. Did you know the back seat of a squad car is wooden and uncomfortably narrow? I tugged to straighten the bulky robe around me and scrunched down on the narrow seat as best I could, hoping no one in town would see me. That was a picture I wouldn't want to see on the news.

My entire body trembled from the inside out every time the image of Poppy Rose's lifeless body sprawled on the bottom of the baptistery popped into my head. To say I was shocked didn't begin to describe the horror of what I'd seen.

How would I break the awful news about Poppy Rose to Miss Nettie? Truly, I didn't want Betsy to learn about any of this until I was cleared of all suspicion. Right now, I had no assurance the evening would end quickly or if I'd even be released. I couldn't rule out the possibility of being an overnight guest in Ruby Springs's local bed-with-bars facility, either. Thinking about that left a knot of anxiety in my stomach. I'd read enough crime novels to know I was bound to be labeled a person-of-interest by the authorities, but I didn't think they could hold me for that reason alone. However, the small, straight-laced community didn't suffer fools kindly, and that included anyone suspected of acting outside the law. I'm pretty sure murder fell into that category with my name at the top of the list of suspects.

Chilled despite the muggy night temperature, I wiggled under the robe to unstick my soggy capris and shirt from various uncomfortable wrinkles and body crevices. By the time we reached police headquarters, I was convinced the miracle I needed wasn't likely to happen. The trail of damp footprints I left followed behind me as I trod barefoot into the building. Back at the church, the investigating team had recovered my sandals and were holding them in a plastic bag as crime scene evidence. *Humph!* What clues could my soggy, faux Crocs possibly give them?

A solemn-faced rookie from the front desk escorted me into a room no bigger than my closet at home, pointed to a chair facing the wall, and left. I surveyed my meager surroundings. Not even one of those two-way mirrors like the cops use in TV crime shows.

Before my shaky legs gave out, I adjusted the robe and pulled out the chair. I didn't feel any better sitting down. In fact, I was a bit light-headed and last thing I wanted to do was pass out in this dismal place. With my luck, I'd wake up in a cell with a couple of loudmouthed streetwalkers.

Not a breath of air stirred inside the tiny area. With no windows, just a long table with a chair on each side surrounded by ugly brown walls, the musty smell lingered everywhere. Old building, old walls, old floors. Dust motes floated past, fanned by my trailing robe. I sneezed three times in succession.

I fidgeted. What was keeping the chief? My watch had stopped working after its own unexpected immersion, but I figured at least an hour had passed since I'd found Poppy Rose. Not that I expected VIP treatment from the police chief or anything, but a cup of hot coffee or a couple of dry towels would've been appreciated. I was only here to answer questions. Nothing to worry about, right?

Too nervous to sit still, I bunched up my borrowed robe to keep from tripping on it and paced the dreary interrogation room while I waited for the chief to make his appearance.

Every time I tried working out the mystery of Poppy's horrible demise in my head, I came up with a big fat zero. Three important pieces of the puzzle were missing—the who, where and why. I searched my memory diligently to find even one of those elusive pieces, but at this point my mind was a jumble. I wanted to cooperate in the investigation, but I wasn't thrilled at being treated like a common criminal. Okay, not a criminal exactly. I hadn't been cuffed. That would've knocked the fine citizens of Ruby Springs right on their sanctimonious keesters and killed any chance of my own personal redemption. NOT what I needed now.

I went back to the chair, which was about as comfortable as sitting on a concrete slab. What was taking so long?

In spite of my bladder's need for relief, I craved caffeine to help steady my wild and crazy nervous system. The thought of looking for a ladies room and a cup of coffee crossed my mind—not that I could leave the room without permission.

As if my thoughts had been intercepted, one of the other sergeants from the squad room stuck his head inside the doorway.

"Ma'am, the chief is ready to see you now."

"Sounds ominous. Am I under arrest?" I was pretty sure I wasn't, but for some reason I needed reassuring to ward off an impending anxiety attack.

"No ma'am. Chief Jackson's just doing his job. Questioning is part of it."

I worried anyway but followed the sergeant through the crowded office area. Ignoring the curious stares of the night staff, I swished past their desks, purple robe flapping behind me like I was royalty. Which, tonight, I definitely was not.

Chapter Four

Around the corner, a big man in a dark blue uniform waited in the doorway of a much larger room than the one where I'd been sequestered. He frowned as I approached. *Uh-oh, not a good sign.* The knot in the pit of my stomach tightened, and my bladder screamed *Let it go! Let it go!*

"Frankie McMasters?" There was nothing friendly in the deep rumble of his voice. Steel gray eyes held my attention as chills rippled through me. My breath caught in my throat. Noah Jackson, Ruby Springs's police chief, towered above my five-feet-four-inch frame by at least a foot. Reason enough not to argue. Why did I feel like I was already on the witness stand? I knew I'd done nothing wrong. Finding Poppy's killer was important to me, too.

"Frankie *Lou*," I corrected, hoping my smile hid my rapidly crumbling confidence. "Everyone calls me by both names."

I stood there, wet and trembling underneath the robe, and waited anxiously for him to make the next move. If he intended to lock me up, he sure was taking his sweet time.

With a brisk nod, he motioned toward a wooden, straight-backed chair. "Please sit down, Frankie *Lou* McMasters. I'm Police Chief Noah Jackson." He took a seat behind a small desk and proceeded to shuffle papers. Even sitting, he was intimidating. Did I mention tall?

Begrudgingly I sat, determined to give brief, straightforward answers and be on my way out the door. Barefooted with my clothes sticking to me like a second skin, I whipped the robe around me with an air of false self-confidence. Thank goodness I wasn't interviewing for a job. Anxiety made my skin prickle and my heart race. I rubbed my arms and swore I would even give up carbs for some dry clothes right now. But not sugar. Never sugar.

The chief scanned the first page, glanced at me, frowned slightly, and scanned the second page. Again he looked up, then back at the papers.

Well, really. Didn't he realize there'd been a murder tonight? Didn't he care? I sniffled. Thinking about Poppy Rose and how she must have suffered brought tears to my eyes. Had she been aware of what was happening to her? Did she try to fight off her attacker? The persistent questions nagged me. Did she drown? My stomach flip-flopped. I wanted answers and wanted them now. I leaned forward in my chair.

"If you don't mind, Chief, could we get on with the questions? I'd like to go home and get out of these wet clothes. Besides, it's a school night, and it's late. My daughter's with a sitter and—" Nervous tension had loosened my tongue, and I babbled senselessly. My ramblings were probably the result of my adrenaline crash, but whatever the cause, a hot shower would do wonders to calm my traumatized mental state.

"I'll make sure you get home safely," he interrupted, "but it may take some time to get through all the questions. Feel free to use the phone on the desk and let your sitter know you'll be late. Offer her extra pay or something but don't mention anything about the accident, understand?"

Was he deliberately ignoring my discomfort? If I hadn't been so miserable, I might have laughed at the thought of Miss Nettie charging for her services like a professional sitter. At the beginning of our arrangement I had offered to pay her for watching Betsy, but she refused to take any money. She loved her role as a stand-in Granny, and she knew my finances were thinner than frog's hair. However, I was uneasy about Betsy's safety and wanted to get home. Tonight's bizarre events made me question the well-being of everyone in this normally quiet community, especially my daughter and Miss Nettie.

"I'm already late," I reminded him again, "and please call me Frankie Lou." Not wanting to aggravate him, I managed to keep my cool, but for goodness sake, couldn't he at least get my name right? I figured he'd be a tough adversary if pushed too far, so the smart thing was for me to stay on his good side. He couldn't know much about me or my past, and I preferred to keep it that way.

Under Chief Jackson's intense scrutiny, I picked up the phone and dialed my neighbor.

Miss Nettie answered on the second ring. "Where in the world are you, Frankie Lou? My goodness, child, you said you'd be here before nine o'clock."

I flinched. "Yes, I know, Miss Nettie, but there's been some trouble at church, and I've been delayed. I'll be a little longer, so would it be all right if Betsy stays overnight at your house? I'll come over and get her tomorrow morning in time to walk her to school."

"Well, my stars, Frankie Lou, of course she can," came her breathless reply. "In fact, she was so tuckered out she's already asleep on the sofa. Now, just what kind of trouble are you having? Are those deacons giving you a hard time? Because if they are, I'll come right over to the church and give 'em a piece of my mind."

Knowing Miss Nettie, she'd do it, too. All I had to do was say the word, and she'd be all over those poor, unsuspecting men like ugly on an ape. But the deacons weren't the problem.

"Oh, you don't have to do that, Miss Nettie. The deacons approved my request. But, uh, there was a slight problem after the meeting, and I'm at the police station now, helping them resolve the matter." I mentally crossed my fingers. Part of what I told her was the truth.

"Trouble? At the church?" Miss Nettie's voice shot up an octave. Shock will do that, you know. I held the phone away from my ear while she continued. "Nobody told me about any trouble. I swan to goodness, how do people think I can print the current church news if they don't tell me what's going on there?"

"Don't worry, Miss Nettie," I interrupted. "I'll be home as soon as I can." Until the police released the information, I wasn't at liberty to tell her Poppy'd had her final baptism by immersion.

"But it's almost midnight. You must be starving. Betsy told me you skipped supper so I made pimento cheese sandwiches for you, plus we baked a double batch of cookies."

I snuck a sideways glance at the chief. His steel gray eyes watched me like a hawk about to snatch a field mouse for his dinner. A cold ribbon of distrust slid down my spine. He arched one eyebrow and tapped the papers on his desk with his forefinger. *Okay, already. I get the hint.*

"That's real sweet of you, Miss Nettie, but I'll have to eat them some other time. Right now, the police chief is waiting for my help. I promise I'll explain everything in the morning, so don't worry. And thanks for taking care of Betsy tonight. I appreciate it."

"Police chief, you say? Well, I declare—"

She was still sputtering when I hung up. I hated being rude to the sweet woman, but what else could I do? I figured I'd have plenty of smoothing over to do tomorrow. Could this night get any worse?

A file folder slid from the desk. The chief swiveled his squeaky chair and bent to retrieve it.

"A squirt of WD-40 would fix that," I offered without thinking.

He ignored my suggestion and opened the folder. Either the irritating squeak didn't bother him or he had a hearing problem.

"Miss Nettie's your baby sitter, that right?"

What did that have to do with Poppy's death? "Well, she's not a hired sitter, exactly. She's my landlady and lives next door, so it's convenient. You see, I work for Doc—"

"The Animal Clinic, yes, I know."

"—Adderly," I continued, ignoring his rude interruption. "Miss Nettie watches my daughter every day after school. She's like a surrogate grandmother. They enjoy each other's company."

"I know that, too," he said, keeping his attention on the contents of the folder. He was a little too smug for a public servant who's supposed to be looking out for the community, if you ask me. Serve and protect should include good manners.

"Part of my job as police chief is making sure all the people under my watch are safe. That would include you, Miz McMasters, as well as Miss Nettie. Since you've only been in town a short time, I'd like you to fill me in on a few more facts."

"Please, just Frankie Lou," I reminded him again. "What facts do you need, Chief Jackson? The officer who brought me here said you had questions about tonight's events, but I've already told Detective Hardy back at the church everything I know. It's plain as day Poppy Rose was murdered. It's your job to find out who killed her."

I was running out of patience. What else could he possibly need from me? I was wet, tired, and hungry and still had a full bladder. Not exactly feeling in a friendly mode.

Chief Jackson pushed out of his chair. In two long strides, he rounded the desk and hitched one hip on the desk top. The look he gave me was serious as sin.

"I'm well aware that Miz Fremont is dead," came his terse reply. "I also know what my job entails. However," his eyes narrowed, "the cause of death and whether or not it was a homicide has yet to be determined. So tell me, why did you return to the church after everyone was gone?" The chief folded his arms across his chest and studied me like I was a bug on a pin.

I squirmed in my seat and sat up a little straighter. I felt like a soggy tea bag. Probably looked like one, too, but at the moment I had other, more pressing issues claiming my attention.

"Like I explained to the detective earlier, I went back to pick up my tote, heard water running, and went to investigate. I had to get into the pool to turn the faucet off. That's when I found Poppy and called 9-1-1." I left out the part about my ungraceful belly-flop. He didn't need that information to solve a murder.

Chief Jackson pulled a yellow pencil from a holder on his desk and twirled it between his fingers like a baton. Humph! And I thought I had nervous habits.

The breath I hadn't realized I was holding came out in a *whoosh*. He stopped the pencil mid-air, but his pause wasn't long enough to calm my own twitching nerves. His incessant quizzing continued. So did the pencil-twirling. Did I mention nerve-twitching? How about wet, cold, and clammy?

"Chief Jackson, would you excuse me a moment while I use the ladies room?"

He rose and motioned to the sergeant standing outside the office door. "Show Miz McMasters the restroom, Sergeant Quincy."

I hurried to follow the sergeant and was back in record time. Chief Jackson looked up from his desk when I entered his office and started right with the questions again before I had a chance to sit down.

"And you've no idea how Miz Fremont got in the baptistery? You didn't hear a scream or any sound other than water running?"

My stars, hadn't I already covered that? I picked at a hangnail on my pinky while stalling for time. Positive his rapid questions were intended to rattle me, I began to reconstruct the chain of events in my mind before I answered. In order to be convincing, I had to keep my facts straight, but that wasn't easy when the voice in my head kept prodding me. *You can do this, Frankie Lou.* My conscience suddenly became my cheerleader.

"All I heard was water running. Like I said, Poppy left the meeting earlier than the rest of us. I stayed to help the deacons clean up. I'm positive her car wasn't in the parking lot when everyone left later. We would've seen it."

"But you came back after that. Why?"

Hadn't he been listening? "I just told you." Worrying that he still doubted my story, I went through the whole thing again, including my side trip to the car dealership. "I hadn't realized my tote bag wasn't with me until I reached for it to get my phone. I wanted to call Miss Nettie and tell her I was on my way home. My phone and all my personal information was in the tote, as well as information about my singers, so I didn't dare leave it at the church overnight. When I got back to the church the lights were on inside the sanctuary, but that didn't worry me. I figured Mr. Hooper, the custodian, was doing a nightly check before locking up. On my way out, I heard water running in the baptistery and went to see what he was doing. No one was there, and the faucet was running full force. In my rush to shut it off, I slipped on the wet steps and fell in. That's how I found Poppy Rose."

Now he knew it all, including my clumsy underwater episode. The lump in my throat made talking painful. The magnitude of the evening's events and the intense questioning overwhelmed me. Was I really a suspect?

I hugged my arms to my chest. The temperature outside was hot and sticky, but underneath the folds of the purple robe, icicles of fear played havoc with my insides. The possibility of being accused of murder had been one of those never-would-happen-to-me thoughts until the chief's interrogation made me face the cold facts of my actions. Yes, I left after the meeting and returned later. No, I couldn't account for the time I spent at the car lot. I had no one to back up my statements. Yes, I was the one who found Poppy's body. Soaking wet like I was, did the chief think I could deny being in the baptistery? Allegedly, I was the only one in the church at the time, but I couldn't prove that fact. The police assumed I was on my way out of the church when they arrived, even though I told them I was waiting for help to get there. Sheesh! Could I have looked any guiltier? Scared by my own thoughts, my shivers shifted into uncontrollable shakes.

"So you called for help because the water was turned on?" He left his perch on the desk and walked across the room to pull a man's blue casual jacket from a wobbly, wooden coat rack.

"Well, yes. I mean, not exactly." A shaky sigh slipped out as I repeated once more how I'd seen Poppy Rose's body on the floor of the baptistery when I was searching underwater for my sandal and had rushed upstairs for my phone to call for help after dragging her out.

The chief walked toward me, his face expressionless, and handed me the jacket.

I thanked him and slipped out of the robe before shoving my arms into the jacket. My damp bottom half still needed covering up so I pulled the robe around me again.

"Sorry we don't keep spare shoes around here." His apology was the second surprise from him in the space of a few minutes. I eyed him warily. Bad cop acting like good cop now?

Back at his desk, he pulled a yellow legal-sized pad from under the jumble of papers. His bold scrawl scratched its way across the page so fast I expected it to burst into flame. *You're not the only impatient person in the room,* I wanted to shout at him.

"Did you meet anyone at the car lot or see anyone on your way there who could verify where you were and when?"

I shook my head. "No one, not until the officers arrived at the church after I called 9-1-1."

"So you're saying the officers arrived shortly after you placed your call from the church, right?" The chief looked up from his note-taking.

"They were there before I hung up. I was so relieved to see them, I didn't ask any questions." Remembering the scary scene when the men in blue burst into the church with guns drawn, I added, "Actually, they didn't give me a chance to say anything."

"Did you see anyone in the church's parking lot when you returned?"

I thought I bit. "Of course! A car! I forgot about the car. I was almost hit when it tore out of the church parking lot. I thought the driver might be Poppy because I thought I saw a pink pillow in the back window."

"You saw a car that might've belonged to the victim and conveniently forgot to mention it? Care to elaborate on how you forgot that bit of information, Miz McMasters?"

"I know it looks bad for me, but I truly did forget about the car until just now. I wasn't sure about the pillow, so I wasn't sure the car was Poppy's, you know? I didn't think it was important at the time. It . . . the car wasn't hers, was it?"

"What about the pillow, please?"

"Miss Nettie told me Poppy always kept the fuzzy pink pillow from her wedding in the rear window of her car. I just assumed . . ."

He waggled the pencil at me. "But it wasn't her, was it? You found her inside—in the baptistery, didn't you? That's what you told Detective Hardy, right?"

"Yes. Yes, that's right. I don't know who was driving, but it looked like her car. I just forgot to mention it to the detective."

Alternately shivering and sweating with funny black spots jive-dancing in my vision, I leaned over and held my head in my hands. *Lord, please don't let me be sick.*

"If we're finished here, Chief, I'd like to go home now."

"Not just yet, Miz McMasters. There was no car in the lot when the police arrived, so how did the deceased get there? That bit of information you conveniently forgot puts a new slant on—"

Detective Hardy strode into the room, interrupting the Chief's grilling. "Afraid the Chief's right, Miz McMasters," he said. "You might want to reconsider your story. There's no record of your call logged in at the emergency response center."

I am so screwed, I thought, right before I passed out.

"WHAT HAPPENED?" I murmured from my hazy world as I cautiously opened one eye. A bright beam of light pierced straight into my brain. *Aghh*! "No light, please!" Squinting, I shaded my eyes with my hand and slowly took in my surroundings. I was lying on a cot, but not in the chief's office.

At the foot of the cot, Detective Hardy, Chief Jackson, and two medics stood staring at me. A third medic kept the intrusive penlight handy, ready to do the deer in the headlights thing again.

A monstrous headache drummed a heavy-metal beat inside my skull. The impact of the detective's last words came back, and I sucked in my breath at the sudden pain. "Am I under arrest?"

"No, but there will be further questioning when you're up to it," Detective Hardy said. "Right now you need to let the medic take a look at you."

The EMT hovering over me looked like a pimply-faced teenager. I cringed.

"You fainted, Miz McMasters," he said. "Your head hit the corner of the desk when you fell. How do you feel now?"

"Are you kidding? Like someone whacked me upside the head with a ball bat, but I don't remember who or why," I muttered. I sounded like I'd been chewing on a bale of cotton. "Mouth's kinda fuzzy, everything's blurry, and my head hurts something fierce right here." I touched the tender spot on my temple and winced. "Outside of that, I'm good. Just take me home."

"Sorry, Miz McMasters, but we have to take you to the hospital first for further observation," the second, older-looking medic said. "Concussions can be serious."

"No!" I pushed up on one elbow, immediately regretting my sudden move when the room spun crazily. "There's nothing wrong with me," I argued, wishing that were true. "I just got too warm, that's all. No need to go anywhere except home. Honestly." I had no medical insurance, and I hadn't eaten anything but sugar, so a trip to the hospital was out of the question.

The men looked at each other and huddled briefly. I strained to listen, but their whispers were too low. Chief Jackson strode over to the cot looking like he was fixing to lay down the law. *Did the man ever smile?*

"Miz McMasters, if you won't agree to go to the hospital, I insist you let them take you to the emergency medical center. A physician there can check you over to make sure you don't have any serious injuries."

"Back up a darn minute! You insist?" Still balanced on one elbow, I squinted at Jackson. It was impossible to talk to him when he kept swaying back and forth. I tried sitting up, but the whole room shifted and blurred when I moved. The waves building in my stomach rolled higher.

"Okay, maybe I'll go to the clinic after all." I eased my spinning head back onto the pillow. "But only for a quick check, understand? Then I'm going home."

Closing my eyes helped a little with the spinning problem, so I kept them shut and focused on hearing what the chief was saying.

He cleared his throat. "By the way," he said, "I called Miss Nettie and informed her you might be staying at the hospital overnight if the doctor decides to keep you for more observation. She said not to worry. She's already put your daughter to bed."

When he turned to leave, I thought I heard him say something about my momma, but the tsunami raised its ugly head just then demanding my attention. I made a pathetic attempt at "Thank you" and grabbed the kidney-shaped basin from the medic.

Chapter Five

Three hours of close scrutiny later by the ER doctors and nurses, I was allowed to leave the Medical Center. A somber-faced Chief Jackson accompanied me outside where a soggy blanket of heat and humidity joined the fatigue already settled on my shoulders. I was roasting in the chief's jacket, but I refused to give it up, since my partially dried clothes still clung to my body's every wrinkle and love handle. I may not be cover girl material, but I darn sure wasn't up for public scrutiny looking like the loser in a wet t-shirt contest. Not that there was anyone in the waiting room at this late hour interested in ogling my body. I pulled the jacket closer, anyway.

The chief took my arm. "Easy does it."

As much as it irked me, I let him help me into the passenger seat of his waiting police cruiser. Grateful to be finished with the doctor's examination and on my way home, I leaned back against the head rest and closed my eyes. At least I didn't have to ride in the back seat. Tired didn't begin to describe the condition of my weary body. The doctor had given me pain medication for my headache and only agreed to release me after the chief assured him someone would be at home to monitor my care. Assuming he had a female member of the police force in mind didn't make me feel any better. The thought of being under the watchful eyes of a stranger gave me the willies. Still, I didn't argue. Yesterday had been way too long, and today didn't look any too promising. I just wanted to go home.

To make matters worse, the detective made no bones about being unhappy about my release. If my call to 9-1-1 was unrecorded, that made me the only person of interest the police had so far. Who made the call that brought the police to the church? I promised the chief and Detective Hardy that I would stay in town. I had no reason to leave. I wanted answers, too.

The image of Poppy Rose's body lying underwater in the baptistery caused an unfamiliar twinge in my heart. Emotions I wasn't prepared to acknowledge threatened my fading composure.

I turned away from the chief when tears snuck out from the corners of my bleary eyes before I could squeeze them back. We made the rest of the trip from the clinic to my house in silence, except for the two times I sneezed.

By the time Chief Jackson parked his cruiser in front of my house, the sun wasn't far from making its morning appearance. As he started to help me out, I eased from his jacket and held it out to him.

"Thanks for the loan, Chief. Sorry you had to work overtime." *Ahchoo!*

"No problem, Miz McMasters." He tossed the jacket on the front seat and followed me up the front steps.

I unlocked the door and started inside, but his firm hand on my arm stopped me.

"I'll go inside first."

I started to object but changed my mind. Arguing was senseless at this point.

The chief stopped just inside the door of the dark living room. "Forget to pay your electric bill?"

"Of course not. I have it auto-paid from my checking account," I said, bristling. "My bills are always paid on time."

I flipped on the wall switch, and the old-fashioned ceiling light squeezed out a pale 40 watt glow. I keep forgetting to replace the bulb in the night light, but a little light was better than none. Some might even call it romantic, but that was the last thing on my mind right now.

Despite the low lighting and the chief's stuffy attitude, my mood lifted the minute I walked inside. My little abode was cool and welcoming, thanks to a brand-new air-conditioning system Miss Nettie had installed after the previous renter skipped off with the old window unit. I dropped my purse on the red thrift-store end table beside the sofa and carried what was left of my mangled lemon bars into the tiny kitchen while the chief took off on an official safety tour of the rest of the house.

Exhausted mentally and physically, I dreaded playing hostess to the Big Man while we waited for his female replacement to arrive. However, the quicker she got here, the sooner he'd leave, and that suited me just fine.

"Sit anywhere, Chief," I said, like there were more choices than the sofa and one very used easy chair. "Would you like coffee while we wait for your replacement?" I asked, hoping he would refuse. "You know, I wasn't aware Ruby Springs had any women on the police force."

He jerked around like he'd been goosed. "Females? Who said anything crazy like that?"

Oops! The words *females* and *police department* obviously didn't belong in the same sentence.

"Why, you did, Chief. I heard you tell the doctor there'd be an adult available to stay with me tonight. The only appropriate replacement would be a female, don't you agree?" I busied myself at the kitchen counter by sorting a pile of mail. No second offer of coffee for him.

"Miz McMasters, let me clear up your misconception. The Ruby Springs Police Department does not have women on the force. I was referring to your mother when I told the doctor Miss Nettie would look out for you until another adult arrived. That was the only way I could get you discharged without staying here myself. And Miss Nettie did say your mother was coming. Now, I'm sorry if that arrangement doesn't meet with your approval. But women cops in Ruby Springs?" He snorted. "Not in a million years."

"In case Miss Nettie forgot to mention it, my momma's in Florida, Chief, so she won't be coming here tomorrow or any other time. In fact, she doesn't even know what's happened tonight." And thank goodness for that, I thought. The idea of Momma showing up in the midst of all this chaos filled me with too-familiar anxiety.

Curious and daring enough to ask, I pursued the touchy subject. "Tell me, Chief, what does the Ruby Springs Police Department have against hiring female police officers?"

The veins in his temple popped up, making me wish I'd left well enough alone.

"For one thing, Miz McMasters, we've never had any female applicants, so that question's never come up. But if it did, there's not a female in this county who could qualify for anything other than answering the phone."

Gosh, tell me how you really feel about women, Chief.

"I had no reason to doubt Miss Nettie when she said your momma would be coming," he continued. "I figured you'd rather go home than stay overnight at the clinic. Would you feel better if I took the assignment?"

"No thanks to both options," I said, barely able to be civil to the man. "To use your own phrase, Chief, not in a million years. And for the record, if my momma had really been aware of my involvement in tonight's unfortunate event, believe me, she would've called the clinic or your office immediately to find out what was going on. That's one fact you can take to the bank."

I wanted him out of my house. Peace and quiet, a hot shower, and a chance to unwind was what I needed. Was that too much to ask? Morning would be here before I was ready for it. I covered a yawn with my hand.

"I'll be fine here on my own, Chief. Really, I will."

His eyebrow raised with a look of skepticism that told me he didn't believe a word I said. His answer surprised me. "All right, I'll leave, Frankie Lou, but only because I know Miss Nettie is right next door and has promised me she'd keep an eagle eye on your place. I know I can trust her to keep her word."

I refused to comment.

Jackson reminded me to lock the door behind him, but he didn't leave until after he'd walked the entire outside perimeter of my house.

I stood watching from the living room window as he drove away and wondered what on earth had prompted his absurd story about Momma coming to visit. Surely he didn't believe Miss Nettie? That whole idea was totally preposterous. I wondered, too, if he realized he'd called me Frankie Lou instead of Miz McMasters? Not that it mattered.

Once the chief left, I tiptoed out the back door and made a quick trip across the yard to Miss Nettie's. One peek inside the living room window was all I needed to assure me Betsy was safely asleep on the sofa with Moses, the cat, curled up at her feet. Back in my tiny galley generally labeled a kitchen, I set the remaining lemon bars on the counter. They were smashed flat as pancakes, but what the heck. They'd taste every bit as delicious as they would have if I'd eaten them at church. But they'd have to wait a little longer. In my state of nervous exhaustion, a chill rippled through me that only a long, steamy shower could fix.

After twenty relaxing minutes underneath the massaging spray of hot water, I felt like a human being again. With only precious hours left before the alarm clock went off at six, I fell into bed, eager for sleep. No such luck!

Thoughts of the upcoming musical fundraising project kept bumping into horrifying underwater images of Poppy. Too exhausted to relax mentally and physically after the evening's terrible ordeal, I gave up on sleep, climbed out of bed, and padded barefoot to the kitchen.

With a bottle of water from the fridge and the remaining lemon bars within easy reach, I settled at the table and opened my handy spiral notebook.

But instead of choosing songs for the next music rehearsal, I wrote down everything I recalled about the events prior to Poppy's death. No matter how hard I tried, I found nothing that pointed to the identity of the attacker. Unfortunately, my impulsive act to save the church from flooding had marked me as a person of interest in what appeared to be a homicide in the eyes of the law. I had to prove my innocence. Trouble was I had no idea where to begin.

An hour later, the only thing I'd finished was the plate of wrecked, leftover lemon bars. On the first page of my notebook, I'd written:

Victim—Poppy Rose deHaven Fremont

1.Scene of crime—origin undetermined, likely baptistery

2.Possible suspects—Norm Watkins—owns local pharmacy—gives me the creeps

3.Brewster Carson—what do I know about this newest deacon?

4.Wilbur Hadley—bachelor, odd sort but seems too nice. Retired? From what?

5.Could Poppy's wacky parents be involved in some way? Why? What would they gain? Insurance?

6.Need to know more about ex-husband Parvis' background. How did he make his millions?

7.Motives of suspects—undetermined. Need more research here

8.My alibi?—None. Zip. Nada. No witness saw me at car dealership. Deacons witnessed argument with Poppy Rose.

9.Find out date and time of funeral service

My notes had nothing to do with the students' vocal group and everything to do with the act of violence that took Poppy's life. The who, where, and why of the horrendous crime against her was something I intended to find out with or without Chief Jackson's help. I was innocent, but the confrontation Poppy and I had in front of the deacons put a nasty slant on the whole incident. Unless the real killer and the motive were found, I might be spending the rest of my life behind bars. I had no clue where to begin, and I'm pretty sure the police didn't either.

How had this tragic event happened and why? More importantly, how would the incident affect my life and Betsy's? Explaining last night's tragedy to Miss Nettie was my first order of business later this morning, but I still had no easy way to describe the event. Right now, my brain needed to shut down so I could get some much needed sleep.

Back in my bedroom, I set the alarm on my cell phone and fell into bed. Tomorrow, today really, the streets of Ruby Springs would be buzzing with the shocking news of tonight's tragedy like a swarm of angry bees. Once again my name would be the target of their painful sting. Not exactly how I had imagined my homecoming.

SLEEP HAD BARELY carried me off to Dreamland before Charlie Daniels and his band charged into my bedroom full blast, leaving my eardrums vibrating to some wild and crazy fiddling while the devil went on down to Georgia.

"I'm in Texas," I mumbled and pulled the pillow over my head. "Not going to Georgia." I burrowed deeper under the covers. The frantic fiddling kept right on until my sleeping brain cells woke up enough to acknowledge the racket coming from my brand-new phone. *Sheesh*! I like Charlie and all that, but yeah, just *sheesh!* That ringtone's gotta go.

Gritty-eyed and a fiddle string away from zero on the Happy Scale, I fumbled around on the night stand until I found the noisy culprit. Squinting, I focused on the blurred name on the Caller ID, but I couldn't see squat without my contacts.

"Hello! Who is this?" I scrambled out of bed and smacked my big toe against the dresser. *Ow! Ow! Double Ow!*

My throbbing toe screamed in protest as I hobbled into the kitchen. Through tears of pain, I stared at the blue digital numbers glowing on the microwave. Really? Four-thirty? In the morning? I'd barely closed my eyes, for cryin' out loud.

"Do you know what time it is?" I shouted at my caller and started back to the bedroom, careful not to bump my sore toe. Whoever was calling could've at least had the decency to wait until a normal hour. After seven-thirty, preferably. Way after. Groaning, I collapsed on the bed and carefully examined my toe. Not broken, after all, but it hurt like—? Nice words failed me.

"Uh, this is . . . mmmm." The caller sounded male, but I didn't recognize the garbled voice.

"Who? Speak up, please." I had no patience for a crank call at this hour.

"Uh, it's Wesley, Miz Frankie Lou." The shaky voice was much clearer now. "You know, Wesley Camps from the singing group? Anyway, I'm real sorry to call so early, but I didn't know who else to ask."

"Ask about what? Wesley?" I bolted off the bed. "What's wrong? Are you in trouble? Where are you?" Holding the phone in one hand, I started pawing through my closet with the other for a clean pair of jeans and a shirt, toe pain ignored.

"I'm home, Miz Frankie Lou, but—"

"Are you hurt? Sick? Is your granny all right? Where's your father?" I wiggled out of my shorty pajamas and tossed them on the bed.

"No ma'am, I'm not hurt. Granny's fine. She went to visit her sister, Aunt EllaMae, in Houston last week, but—" He hesitated, his voice wobbling again. "My dad's at the police station right now, Miz Frankie Lou. They came and took him downtown. Claimed he was in a fight at Murphy's last night and damaged some stuff. I swear he didn't do it, Miz Frankie Lou. Honest! He was right here at home."

Wesley and his granny lived in the trailer park on the west side of town. Murphy's Tavern is across town in the older part of Ruby Springs, east of the railroad tracks. Its clientele consists mostly of bikers passing through to avoid the freeway and the usual number of rowdy locals. Rumor has it there's illegal private entertainment of some sort going on in the back of the establishment, but I don't know that for a fact.

"What was your father doing over at Murphy's, Wesley? And who was he fighting?"

"That's why I'm calling, Miz Frankie Lou. He never left the house last night. I need to tell that to the police chief. When those two policemen came here to get him, I told them he was home all night, but they didn't believe me. They took him downtown, anyway. I didn't know who to call until I thought of you. I hope you're not mad at me."

"Of course I'm not mad at you, Wesley, but hang on a minute, will you?"

In my hurry I'd tugged on my jeans, but my head was stuck partway through the neck of my knit top. I put the phone down and quickly shoved my arms through the sleeves, pushed my head the rest of the way through the neck, and zipped my jeans. Sliding my bare feet into a pair of red flip-flops, I grabbed the phone again.

"Okay, now start at the beginning. You say your dad was taken to police headquarters this morning?"

"Yes, Miz Frankie Lou, about an hour and a half ago, but I know he didn't start a fight. He wasn't even at Murphy's. Besides, he's tryin' real hard to find a job and stay out of trouble. I really need to go to the police station and see if he's okay. Could you take me? Please?"

Did he think I'd refuse? The worry in the boy's voice tore at my heart. I didn't blame him for being scared.

"Of course I'll take you, Wesley. I'll pick you up as soon as I let Miss Nettie know where I'm going. Betsy stayed with her last night so I need to give her a quick call. Give me fifteen minutes, okay?"

His deep sigh of relief came through loud and clear. "Thanks, Miz Frankie Lou. I owe you big time."

"Never mind. Just give me your address and be ready when I get there." Not sure what I was getting into, I only knew I wasn't going to ignore Wesley's plea for help.

After writing down the information he gave me, I dialed Miss Nettie. She answered on the third ring.

"Miss Nettie, I have to go downtown again," I said and hurriedly explained Wesley's call.

"Don't worry about Betsy, hon, but you be careful," she warned. "I've only seen Joe Camps around town a time or two. Seems nice enough, but you never can tell. Spending that many years behind bars is bound to change a man some." She proceeded to give me a condensed version of what she thought I should know about Wesley's father. Wrongfully charged and sentenced for a crime he didn't commit, Joe Camps was eventually acquitted after serving time in prison. Miss Nettie would've kept on talking, but I finally told her I needed to hang up so I could leave.

Grateful for her concern, I assured my neighbor I'd be careful, thanked her for letting Betsy spend the night, and hung up without ever learning why Joe Camps had gone to prison in the first place.

As I drove to the trailer park to pick up Wesley, I went over everything she'd related to me. According to her, Joe had been released from prison about six months ago. During the years he was incarcerated, Joe's momma, Granny Camps, took in Wesley, and the two lived in a used, single-wide park model in the Ruby Springs Trailer Park, a decent but small community on the west side of town. After his release, Joe started looking for a job so he could provide a bigger, better place for them to live. For now they were still crowded into Granny Camps's very small house trailer. Strangely enough, the upright, church-going business owners in Ruby Springs didn't have any jobs available for Joe.

Wesley had never spoken much about his father except to say no one in Ruby Springs wanted to hire an ex-con. I was pretty sure starting a barroom brawl wasn't the way to find a job, either, but I couldn't let Wesley deal with this situation alone. With his Granny out of town, he needed someone to stand by him. As if last night's tragedy wasn't enough to worry me, I had Wesley counting on my help, too.

When we walked into police headquarters thirty minutes after he'd phoned me, every uniformed person in the room looked up from their desks. I marched right up to a long counter with a wooden INFORMATION sign on it. A burly sergeant took his time coming to see what we wanted.

"Something I can help y'all with, ma'am?" His sleepy Texas drawl told me he'd pulled the all-night shift, but I didn't recognize him from my earlier visit.

"Yes, this boy's father was brought in last night, and he'd like to see him." I had no idea what the protocol was for such a visitor or if Joe had already been taken to the county jail across town, but I was game to try anything.

"His name's Joe Camps," Wesley added, stuffing his nervous hands in his pants pockets.

The sergeant keyed the information Wes gave him into a computer. After staring at the monitor a minute or two, he looked up. "According to this, you'll need to see the chief first." He stepped out from behind the counter and motioned for us to follow. "This way."

Facing Chief Jackson again had my nerves tangled in a knot, especially since Joe Camps was the reason for my second visit tonight. I already had more black marks against me than I could erase. Dragging my feet, I watched Wesley run down the hall to keep up with the sergeant. They stopped just as the door to the chief's office opened. My own steps came to an abrupt halt. I stared, wide-eyed, as the last person on earth I expected to see again tonight scurried out of the chief's office.

Chapter Six

The older man kept his head down and shoulders hunched, but that didn't stop me from recognizing him. No one else in Ruby Springs wore outlandish bow ties and looked like a bald-headed garden gnome.

"Why, hello there, Mr. Hadley," I said loud enough to make him look up. "What brings you here so early this morning?"

Since I was practically standing in his path, the deacon either had to stop and talk or run into me. He hesitated just long enough to make me wonder if he was about to do the latter. I didn't know him well, but he'd been polite enough at the meeting. He did get a bit over-excited when my sweet tea baptized Poppy Rose.

"Oh, Fr . . . Frankie Lou," he stuttered. His gaze darted from side to side before finally landing on his own feet. "I, uh, had an urgent matter to discuss with the chief. Yes, urgent." He avoided eye contact with me—a sure sign the man was lying.

Before I could question the deacon further, Chief Jackson gave the man a hearty pat on the shoulder and urged him down the hall again.

"No need to explain to Miz McMasters, Wilbur. Everything's taken care of." the chief said. "Be careful on your way home, y'hear?"

He waved the nervous man on and turned back to where Wesley and I waited in front of his office. "Didn't expect to see you here again so soon, Miz McMasters. As to your question for Mr. Hadley, his reason for being here was legitimate. Nothing you need to worry about." He ushered us into the room. "Now, I understand you've asked to see Joe Camps? Do you know the man?"

The shock of seeing Deacon Hadley in such an unlikely place had momentarily thrown me off guard. I'd barely gathered my thoughts again before Chief Jackson hurried the deacon off like the two of them had something to hide. A conspiracy? I shook my head. I really had to stop imagining crazy things.

Until now, Wesley had been fidgeting while he waited impatiently beside me and the sergeant. When he stepped forward to speak to the chief, the sergeant placed a restraining hand on his shoulder.

"Never mind, Wesley," I said, glaring at the sergeant. "I'll explain to Chief Jackson."

Wesley shrugged the hand off his shoulder. "No, ma'am. It's my place to do that." He turned to the chief. "Sir, it was me who asked Miz Frankie Lou to bring me down here so I could talk to my dad. His name is—"

"I know who your father is, son, but I'm afraid you can't see him. Unless you've got money to pay his fine, he'll be staying here until the paperwork is finished and he's transferred to the county jail. You understand?"

"But I know he didn't start any fight, sir. He was home with me all night, I swear. He doesn't want to go back to prison. If I promise to bring you my next paycheck from Thornton's Market, will you let him go now?"

Chief Jackson's answer was a flat and unsympathetic "No."

Heartless man, I thought. Couldn't he see Wesley was only trying to help his dad?

"If Wesley says his dad was at home, what proof do you have that Mr. Camps was at the tavern or even started the fight?" I challenged the chief, though after the way he evaded my question about Deacon Hadley, I wasn't too hopeful of gaining any information about Joe Camps.

"Miz McMasters, this is police business. Don't worry your pretty little head about what doesn't concern you. Now, why don't you mozey on back home and let me handle matters here?"

My pretty little head? Mozey? *Grrrr!* The man was incorrigible.

"My dad didn't start no fight!" Wesley insisted. "Why won't you let me see him?"

"Try to calm down, Wesley," I urged softly. "We'll get to the bottom of this in a minute."

With all that had happened within the last few hours, *bizarre* was the only word I could think of to describe the evening's crazy events. The list was a long one. Finding Poppy Rose's body in the baptistery, my questioning at the police station and my missing emergency call for help, Miss Nettie claiming Momma was coming to Ruby Springs, Wilbur Hadley leaving Chief Jackson's office just a few minutes ago, and this whole weird thing with Wesley's dad, Joe Camps . . . could anything else possibly go wrong?

As if God heard my question, His answer came through a call on the chief's desk phone.

Noah Jackson picked up his phone. "Yeah, yeah. Well, hell. Okay, thanks. I'll take care of it." Clearly displeased, he dropped the phone in place and looked at Wesley with a shake of his head. "Looks like your daddy's going home with you this morning, after all, kid. Why didn't you tell me his brother was back in town?"

Brother? Joe Camps had a brother?

"I tried," Wesley said, "but you wouldn't give me a chance." He took a deep breath, choosing his words carefully. "Uncle Jess showed up two days ago. My dad didn't want him around, but Uncle Jess, he stayed at the trailer anyway 'cause Granny was gone. He knew she would've chased him off with her broom if she'd been home. Most of the time when he wasn't drinking, he slept on the couch. My dad tossed him out yesterday afternoon. Said he was nothing but trouble and told him not to ever come back. Uncle Jess was madder than a rained-on rooster when he left. Told my dad he'd get even. Guess that's what he tried to do by blaming him for the fight, huh?"

"And almost got away with it, too." Chief Jackson commented. "Your uncle's just been identified as the guy who started the fight at Murphy's. He's being brought in now. Seems when the bar owner tried to get him to pay for the damages caused by the brawl your uncle claimed to be Joe Camps, gave your grandmother's address, and told the owner to send him a bill. Then he high-tailed it out of there before Murphy called us. We found your dad at home and brought him in for questioning. Natural mistake. No big deal. All's well that ends well, huh, kid?"

No big deal? My mouth must've been hanging open in disbelief. Chief Jackson had blown off the department's goof-up like it wasn't important. What kind of justice was this?

"I'll make sure your dad gets a proper apology." He gave Wesley a pat on the shoulder. "Sorry, kid."

Wesley pulled away. "You profiled my dad," he accused the Chief, not ready to forgive the mistake so easily. "You knew my dad had a prison record and figured he was guilty of fighting even when he hadn't been out of the house. He didn't have any marks on him like he'd been fighting, either. He's not a bad guy. He never was. Nobody believed he was innocent back eight years ago, and nobody believes it now. It's not fair!" With a ragged sob, this big, tender-hearted kid who'd never had a decent break in his young life turned aside to knuckle away the tears sliding down his face.

Bullying comes in many varieties. I was well acquainted with the one Wesley Camps had just witnessed. Profiling is a lot like being branded, and it wasn't always fair. I wanted to give Wes a hug but knew it would've embarrassed him. Instead, I gave him an encouraging smile and a nod to let him know I was proud of him. After the Chief left the room, I hugged him anyway.

We sat together quietly and waited for Joe Camps to be released from the overnight holding cell. At least he hadn't been sent to the long-term lockup on the other side of town. Aside from providing Wesley and his dad with a ride home, supporting Wesley was the least I could do. The wait gave me plenty of time to wonder how thorough the investigation of Poppy Rose's death would be.

Would my own innocence be as difficult to prove as I'd expected? After all, I had no one to back up my alibi, and there were seven deacons who witnessed the argument I'd had with the victim on the very night of her death. Would God send another surprise to get me out of my predicament, or would I have to save myself this time? At this rate, even a five-gallon bucket of polish wouldn't be enough to make my halo shine before it slid right off my head and landed in a nasty puddle of gossip.

"THANKS FOR COMING to my rescue." Joe Camps said later as he climbed into the back seat of my minivan beside his son and pulled the door shut.

"You're welcome, Mr. Camps. Glad I could be of help."

"Well, I appreciate your kindness, ma'am. And call me Joe."

I looked up and caught a glimpse of him in the rear view mirror. For the umpteenth time, I found myself justifying my curiosity about him as simply concern for Wesley. Yeah, right.

I'd heard one of The Joyful Noise girls use the phrase "totes adorbs" to describe a good-looking guy. That surely did describe Joe Camps. Rough around the edges, yet the softness in his eyes when he looked at his son didn't fit the profile of a criminal. Not at all how I'd imagined Wesley's father would look. I didn't have a firm image pre-planted in my head, mind you. I don't believe in profiling, but he was an ex-con, had spent time in prison, even though his acquittal was a point in his favor. Our eyes met for one brief moment. He angled his head, raised an eyebrow.

Embarrassed at being caught watching him, I jerked my attention back to driving and pulled out into the street. There was very little traffic this early, thank goodness. No one to see me at the police station a second time and add fuel to the fire I'd started when I found Poppy Rose's body. *Lord, you gave me a mountain when you know I'm afraid of heights. I'm gonna need some help.*

"Dad, why didn't you tell the cops Uncle Jess was in town when they came after you, anyway?" Slumped down in the back seat, Wesley asked the same question that bothered me. A bar wasn't the best place for a recently released felon to visit. Why wouldn't he deny the charge if he hadn't been there?

When Joe glanced into the rearview mirror, he caught me staring . . . again. Darn it! I slowed down at the intersection and waited for the red light to change.

"I made a mistake, son. I thought the cops would believe me when I told them I wasn't there. Didn't think your Uncle Jess being in town would make a difference. Boy, was I wrong." Joe took his cap off and raked a hand through his sandy brown hair and—

Oh, no! I swear something crazy happened inside my sinfully shameful brain. Tingles started zinging from the top of my head to the tips of my curled toes.

I ordered my misbehaving mind to *Stop that right now and take this man home!* The conversation going on in the back seat of the van was impossible not to hear. Really, it was.

"But you weren't at the bar," Wesley was saying, "so why'd you let Uncle Jess make trouble again?" The sting of his disappointment was clearly evident in the boy's voice. "You could've been sent back to prison."

I shouldn't be hearing this discussion. Still, if they were talking loud enough for me to overhear Joe's answer, it wasn't my fault, was it?

"Never figured Jess would get in a bar fight after I made him leave the house, son. How was I to know he'd pretend to be me?"

Wesley shrugged. "Why wouldn't he? He's blamed you before for stuff you didn't do. Didn't you learn anything when you were in prison?"

I glanced in the rearview mirror just as Joe's head snapped around. "Who've you been talking to, Wes?"

The car behind me honked impatiently, and I quickly turned the corner and headed for the trailer park. Slumped down in the back seat, Wesley refused to answer his father's question. My disappointment at that decision surprised me. Why should I care about Joe Camps's problems? Didn't I have my own battles to fight right now?

I pulled into the entrance to the park and turned right at the second corner. The Camps' single-wide home was located on Sunflower Lane, but that was a big joke. Not a single sunflower grew anywhere among the cluster of modest mobile homes on either side of the street. Instead, a single row of scraggly pink begonias bloomed along the cracked sidewalk leading to Granny Camps's trailer. A metal wind chime jingled softly from a black shepherd's hook stuck in the ground next to the steps.

Wesley jumped out of the van as soon as it came to a stop. He tossed a quick "Thanks for the ride, Miz Frankie Lou," over his shoulder and took off up the metal steps into the trailer before his dad had a chance to say anything.

I waited for Joe to get out of the van, not quite sure what else to say to him. After all, our introduction tonight had been awkward, to say the least. He stopped at my window. When he tapped, I pushed the button and opened it. Early-morning stubble made a rough shadow along his strong jawline. Weariness made his brown eyes darker, his manner quieter, more respectful, yet beneath all that I sensed a defensive side of him that he kept tightly in check. A ticking time bomb? Oh, I hoped not, for Wesley's sake.

"I appreciate the ride and want to apologize again for the inconvenience, ma'am. Thanks for being so nice to my son, too. Wesley speaks mighty highly of you and what you're doing for him and his friends. They're a good bunch of kids, you know. I've heard 'em sing, too, and well, they sure do a fine job when they set their mind to it. They'll make you proud."

He backed away from the window and stood there all of two seconds before he touched the brim of his well-worn Dallas Cowboys gimme cap with a two-fingered salute. "Ya'll take care now." He went into the trailer without a backward glance.

"Well, for goodness sakes." Puzzled, yet certain there was nothing else to do, I headed for home. The night had been a tragedy, and this morning had begun on a sour note, as well. I dreaded the long day ahead, fearing it would bring more of the same.

"Lord, give me strength," I prayed silently when I reached home. Too wired to try napping for the few minutes before I had to take Betsy to school, I filled the coffee maker and sat down at the kitchen table to wait for it to brew. I had some explaining to do, but no answers for the questions Miss Nettie was bound to ask when she brought Betsy home.

I had plenty of questions of my own, and mulled them over in my uneasy mind. How could I clear my name as a person of interest? I needed to find the *who* and *why* before the chief hauled me in for questioning again. And now there was my unexpected connection with Joe Camps, an ex-con with a shady brother. That didn't help my situation.

As much as I disliked Poppy Rose, I would never wish her or anyone such a brutal death. And why Poppy? Had she drowned in the baptistery or was she dead before she'd been pushed down the steps into the water? I hoped she hadn't known the horror of drowning. My personal opinion? With all that duct tape around her, the act had to be premeditated. How could the chief and his detective not know this?

Frustrated, I left the table, stretched out the kinks in my back and walked across the room to stare out of the window.

I stood there, watching the sunrise, contemplating the uncertainty of our time on Earth and vowing to make my own allotted days count for something beneficial to everyone. Maybe finding Poppy Rose's killer would add a gleam to my tarnished reputation. Lord knows I needed all the help I could get with that project.

I'd barely finished showering after a much-needed jolt of caffeine and was donning clean capris to go with a red knit top when I heard a knock. Zipping up, I hurried to open the door. My neighbor and Betsy stood there waiting, Miss Nettie holding a tray with a coffee pot and plate of something wrapped in foil. Betsy was sleepy-eyed and still in her pajamas.

"We're early, but Betsy was anxious to see her momma," Miss Nettie announced in a no-nonsense tone that told me my daughter wasn't the only impatient one. "Coffee's ready, and I brought fresh cinnamon buns, too. There's plenty of time for you to tell me everything. And I mean EVERYTHING!"

Betsy flew into my arms and hugged me tight. "Hi, Momma, I'm glad you're home."

"I'm glad, too, sugar," I said, planting a smooch on her cheek and holding her close until she wiggled out of my arms with an impatient protest. "Did you have fun with Miss Nettie?"

"Yes ma'am, but I wish it was time for camp now. I'm tired of school." She snuck a cinnamon bun from under the cover of the plate Miss Nettie held and slid a look my way. I grinned at her impish trick.

"Only one more week, hon. Right now it's time for breakfast, so run along and get dressed. It's already seven, and your classes start at nine." I smoothed her tangle of dark curls, the only legacy B.J. had left his beautiful daughter that made me happy and sad at the same time.

"Camp's gonna be so much fun, Momma. Thanks for letting me

go." She bounded down the hall to her room. Anticipation of her first week-long adventure without me had her bubbling with excitement. Not me. I missed her already, knowing I would suffer a big case of lonely while she was gone. I'd had some serious second thoughts about her extended visit with her grandparents this summer.

My van would never make it to Florida, but the church campgrounds were only twenty miles away, close enough to get there in case of an emergency. The Joyful Noise singers would be making their first public appearance in two weeks, and that had occupied most of my thoughts this past week, but today the investigation of Poppy's death loomed over me like a black cloud of doom. Finding Poppy's killer and clearing my name as a suspect was uppermost in my mind. The to-do list inside my head kept getting longer. Every day I added more and more to it.

There's also the matter of keeping my boss, Doc Adderly, happy. I desperately needed my job at the clinic in order to pay for life's simple needs like rent, food, and sending Betsy to church camp. *Hello God, it's me again, Frankie Lou.* What with my situation so iffy, maybe I should just keep her home. Then again, I don't want to expose her to a lot of ugly gossip over the whodunit to Poppy Rose.

"I swan, Frankie Lou, are we going to stand here all morning while the coffee gets cold?" My neighbor stood in the doorway impatiently tapping her foot. The insistent tone of her voice rescued me from my mental agonizing and back to the front door with a jolt.

"Oh, of course not, Miss Nettie. Come on in."

"Humph! About time." Miss Nettie shoved the plate of baked goods into my hands. "I've been frettin' and stewin' over that Breaking News bulletin on TV late last night. You have plenty of explaining to do. Figured you could do with a little something special after such an awful time last night."

"You mean the lack of sleep? Oh, I'm—"

"You know very well I'm not talking about sleep. Now get yourself in the kitchen and tell me what's going on!"

Miss Nettie marched right past me with her coffee pot. "By the way, missy, your eyes look like two pieces of red-hot coal. You need to get more sleep."

Puzzled by her strange remarks, I hurried to the kitchen for coffee mugs and plates. I needed her strong coffee in the worst way. She spoke as I took the dishes from the cupboard.

"You know, Frankie Lou, I wasn't too worried when you told me there'd been a little trouble, but when I saw you with the police in that news video last night . . . Saints alive! I had to call your momma. I knew you'd want me to."

"What?" I spun around so fast I almost walloped her with the dishes in my hands. "Miss Nettie, please tell me you're joking." I'd noticed the reporter with a camera in the crowd at the church. Dang it! Even worse than a single photo, he'd filmed an entire video. Now the whole town will think I was involved in the crime. And Miss Nettie had actually called Momma. I looked Heavenward. *Lord, how do I get myself into these predicaments?*

"I don't joke about murder!" Her silver-gray curls bobbed with each word she spoke. "It won't take long for everyone to figure out that information. Something like this is big news in our little corner of Texas."

I put the dishes on the table before I dropped them and pulled out a chair. *Take a deep breath, Frankie Lou. She means well even if her porch light's on sometimes when nobody's home.* "Miss Nettie, what made you call Momma? You do remember Momma lives in Florida, don't you?"

"I'm not senile, child. Of course, I remember. But you didn't tell me somebody died!"

"Who told you someone died?" I could barely speak around the ball of fear stuck in my throat.

Miss Nettie looked at me then like I should've answered my own question.

"Why, when I saw that Breaking News flash on the late night news after you went to fetch Wesley, I knew you'd want me to call her. The police said there'd been an accident earlier last night at Faith Community involving a 'prominent member' of Ruby Springs's society. The video showed the police hustling you away from a gurney with a body on it. It was obvious you weren't in the body bag. I figured the rest out for myself. Lucky I phoned your momma. There's a news flash on *Good Morning, America* this morning, too, so sooner or later those gossipy biddies would've called her. They keep her informed of every little thing that happens in town."

My neighbor had done exactly what she accused the 'biddies' of doing.

"She's coming sooner than y'all had planned. Said she didn't want Betsy to be exposed to your personal crisis. Those are her words, mind you, not mine. She figured on booking a night flight to get here right away. I 'spect she'll show up sometime later today. She didn't say anything about meeting her plane, but I reckon you might have to pick her up at the airport. She'll probably call you when she gets to the DFW airport." Miss Nettie tapped her empty cup with one finger and bobbed her head toward the coffee pot.

I filled her cup and grabbed one of the sugary cinnamon buns for myself, stuffing a big bite in my mouth to keep from saying something I'd be sorry for later. There was no way my van would make it to the Dallas airport and back home, even if Miss Nettie was telling the truth and Momma paid for gas. A fortune teller with a dirty crystal ball could see my future wasn't looking too pretty.

It's a well-known fact that everyone in Ruby Springs watches *The Early Reporter* every morning and noon. The local television news program comes out of a neighboring city and naturally, the station monitors the police reports in the surrounding small communities like Ruby Springs. I wasn't sure how much information the police had released to the media so far, but I knew better than to argue with this shorter-than-five-foot, silver-haired, steel magnolia bringing me much needed high-octane morning coffee.

Miss Nettie meant well, sure, but sometimes her good intentions made me want to bang my head against the wall in frustration. Momma's the one person I didn't need or want here right now. I slumped back in my chair. "You really did call her?"

Avoiding my eyes, she nodded. "I was only trying to do the right thing."

"But why, Miss Nettie?"

"Because you were in trouble, and I thought she should know before she saw it on television. After all, she is your momma." Sniffing loudly, Miss Nettie drew herself up, all indignant and martyr-like.

Oh, great. Now I've gone and hurt her feelings. The explosion building inside my head climbed to the top of the Richter scale, but my spirits dropped lower than a snake's belly for causing my neighbor such distress.

"Never mind, Miss Nettie. Our plans aren't changing," I said, guilt-ridden for scolding her. "Momma knows Betsy's already signed up to leave for camp as soon as school's out next week. She'll visit my parents in July, just the way we planned. After camp and not before." I topped off our cups and took a deep gulp from mine. Caffeine couldn't hit my veins fast enough this morning.

Miss Nettie took another sip. "When I told her Betsy was spending the night with me because you'd been taken to the police station, she threw a five-star conniption fit. There was nothing I could say to change her mind. I swan, Frankie Lou, that momma of yours would've been here in an instant if she'd had wings."

"Or a broom," I muttered under my breath.

My heavy heart lifted when one corner of Miss Nettie's mouth twitched, her hearing obviously not impaired in the least. I'd been forgiven.

"But I wasn't really arrested, you know. The police haven't declared the death a homicide."

"Didn't matter to her. She was determined to come." Miss Nettie returned to her coffee, satisfied now that she'd done no wrong.

"I know you're right, but I'm still surprised Daddy let her come all this way by herself. That's not like him."

"Well, the way she carried on over the phone, you'd have thought you were already on your way to jail wearing an orange jumpsuit and flip-flops and Betsy was headed to a foster home. What a bunch of hooey! If I told her once, Frankie Lou, I told her four times she didn't need to come because we could handle everything just fine, but your momma's got a real stubborn streak. I tried my best to talk her out of coming, child, I really did, but she simply wouldn't listen. So I guess you'd better tell me the rest of the details about last night before she gets here. That way, I can defend you."

"I don't need defending, Miss Nettie. I haven't done anything wrong."

"Then why'd the police take you to headquarters and question you for hours? Child, you'd better do a good job of explaining before your momma shows up. I'll need to know everything that's happened if you expect me to back up your alibi."

"What on earth did the reporter say on the news announcement? Did they identify the victim?"

"No, but it didn't take much to figure that out after I spoke with Deacon Botts last night. I was worried when you called. I told your momma it looked like Poppy Rose had been murdered right there in Faith Community Church. What did Chief Jackson and the detective have to say? You'd better have a solid alibi, Frankie Lou. Most of the cops in this town are as useless as hip pockets on a hog. They'll lock you up and toss away the key if they think that'll get them a promotion. You do have an alibi, don't you?"

"All I have for an alibi is my word. I left the church and stopped at Deals on Wheels to daydream. That's when I realized I didn't have my tote, so I went back to the church."

Miss Nettie did an eye-roll. "Well, that'll get you top billing on the suspect list unless someone can vouch for your whereabouts after you left the church. You say you went to the Deals on Wheels lot on the way home, huh? What about security cameras? There have been several cars stolen off Griff Hollender's lot recently. He's bound to have some installed around the place. That night's film should show Noah Jackson you were there."

"The police would've already checked that out since I told them I'd been there." Surely they weren't as incompetent as Miss Nettie inferred.

"You sure didn't help yourself any by showing up at the police station with Joe Camps's son so soon after finding Poppy, either. Did you have to spring him out of jail?"

"He wasn't in jail, Miss Nettie. They were still questioning him when the chief got a phone call to release him. Seems Joe's brother was the one who got in a fight and wrecked the bar. By the time Murphy got it figured out and called the police, the brother was gone. Chief Jackson let Joe go home. They were bringing his brother in."

Miss Nettie clucked her tongue. "Jess Camps always was a troublemaker. Wouldn't surprise me none it he had something to do with Poppy's murder."

I shook my head. "That seems a little far-fetched, doesn't it? Why would Joe's brother want to kill Poppy? I think someone had a grudge against her. Someone who knew she'd be at the church last night."

Miss Nettie slapped her hands on the table. "Ha! So you admit the body in the bag was Poppy Rose. See? I told you I'd figured it out."

Oh, shoot! I hadn't meant to let that slip. "Don't say anything, please. If the police think I've revealed any names before they release their report to the public, they'll have me locked up for sure." When would I learn to keep my mouth shut?

"Well, like I said, I did mention to your Momma that I thought the victim was Poppy Rose, but I promise not to say any more until after the public police report. Meantime, you'd better start figuring out what you plan to do next."

"Next? Well, right now I'm going to get Betsy's cereal and toast ready. She's got thirty minutes before we have to leave. Please don't mention any of this to Betsy. I don't want her to worry about me or Poppy Rose's unfortunate accident."

"Humph! That was no accident. I ought to go down and offer my services to Chief Jackson. I could tell him a thing or two that might help get to the bottom of this case. Not much goes on around town that I don't know about."

I didn't doubt that for a minute. Just the thought of her getting involved in the chief's investigation gave me a nervous twitch in my eye. "Oh, Miss Nettie, that's not a good idea." I knew from past experience that her idea of helping usually resulted in disaster.

A car horn blared as I was reaching for the box of cereal in the cupboard, and Betsy went racing past me.

"Somebody's here!" She opened the front door and yelled back, "It's Grammy! Momma, Grammy's here!"

My hands flew up like I'd been smacked with a Taser, scattering the entire box of crunchy chocolate-cinnamon flavored cubes all over the kitchen floor.

Usually, any kind of surprise gets a semi-startled reaction from me. This particular surprise hit me right between the eyes. She whirled through the house and into my kitchen like a well-groomed tornado, not a wrinkle anywhere in her bright yellow slacks and coordinated top. All I could do was stare in amazement. Who was this woman and where was my real momma?

Chapter Seven

I held my tongue as this new Florida retiree, aka Momma, parked her gaudy, oversized, shell-and-palm-tree-decorated straw handbag on the kitchen table and marched across the linoleum floor, wooden-heeled green and yellow sandals clicking like bad-fitting dentures.

"Well now, what's this nonsense I heard about you being hauled off to jail, Frances Louise? What on earth have you done now?" She stopped right in front of me, hands planted on her hips and delivered her question in her best Stern Momma tone. Not even a "hello" first.

"Hey, Momma," I croaked. Sudden surprises make my voice all wonky, too. I cleared my throat and continued. "I'm sorry you got the wrong impression about what happened at church. I wasn't 'hauled off.' I only went to the police station to help them out by answering a few questions. It was late when we finished, and Miss Nettie was kind enough to keep Betsy overnight. There's no reason for you to get in a huff about that. Everything's under control. You didn't have to come."

Lord, you better hurry up with that help. I need it sooner than expected—like now.

I probably should explain that ever since she and Daddy retired to Florida, Momma's become a lot more independent and outspoken than she was when I was growing up. I'm not quite sure what brought about her transformation. As the minister's wife she never wore anything but ultra-conservative dresses when we lived in the parsonage. Never made a decision without asking for Daddy's approval, either, if my memory serves me right.

Now, out of the blue, she's come all the way from Florida back to Ruby Springs by herself, dressed like a South Beach socialite on a Walmart budget, of all things. She's sixty years old, for goodness sakes. Not sixteen. Besides, she never went anywhere without Daddy unless you counted the weekly Women's Bible Circle meetings at church. Even then, Daddy was usually in his office in the church annex. I didn't even know she knew how to drive until I was thirteen. In those days, Daddy occupied the driver's seat in more ways than one.

Momma said "*Humph!*" like she didn't believe a word I said and turned her attention to Betsy with a hug. I was proud of the way Betsy held still while Momma squeezed the daylights out of her only grandchild.

When all the hugging finally ended, Miss Nettie, bless her heart, took Momma by the arm and steered her into the kitchen, where she proceeded to push her into a chair and shove a cup of coffee under her nose, same as she'd done to me a few minutes earlier.

"Here you go, Louisa, fresh coffee. Now then, tell us all about your trip. I don't think Frankie Lou was expectin' you so soon." Miss Nettie slid a blue-eyed, sideways glance my way and winked. The old sweetie knew darn well Momma's arrival had momentarily rendered me speechless. I helped myself to another much-needed sip of caffeine. Someone ought to sell that stuff in its pure form. Oh wait! I think someone already has.

Momma *tsk-tsk'd* then, same as always when something didn't set right with her. "Nettie, thank you for informing me of my daughter's trouble with the police. And at the church of all places." Another *tsk*. "Naturally, I got here as fast as I could. As her momma, it's my duty to be here in her hour of need."

My second jolt of coffee snorted out through my nose. "Hour of need?" I coughed and bolted down the hall to the bathroom for a tissue.

"Oh, I never said you needed her, Frankie Lou," Miss Nettie called after me.

Three minutes later I was back in the kitchen ready to put my foot down. "Momma, I don't have an hour of need. Truly. I'm not in trouble with the law, either, so there's nothing for you to take care of. I'm sorry you made your trip for nothing."

I know that sounds tacky, but sometimes Momma's good intentions fall a mile or two short of their target.

Momma bristled like a poked-at porcupine but never said a word—just gave me her version of The Look.

"I don't mean to sound ungrateful, Momma. You know we're glad to see you. You surprised me, that's all." Any minute now I expected bumps to appear on my tongue for lying. I glanced at the clock. Almost time for Betsy to leave for school and for me to make an appearance at the clinic if I wanted a paycheck this week, which I did. Want a paycheck, that is.

"We'd love to stay and hear what your plans are, Momma, but Betsy and I have to leave right after breakfast. Why don't you tell us now while

I check to see what other kind of cereal I have?"

Sometime in the midst of the chaos, Miss Nettie had magically cleaned up the mess on the floor.

I mouthed a *thank you* as I passed her on my way to the fridge, where I promptly stuck my head inside and pretended to hunt for something important—like an excuse to send Momma back to Florida on the next flight out of Dallas.

"So you rented a car at the airport, Momma?" I asked, digging through the crisper and coming up with a tomato that had seen better days. I tossed it in the garbage, grabbed the carton of orange juice, and set it on the counter.

She snorted. "Well, of course, I did. It would've taken me too long to drive here from Florida. Didn't I tell you your father drove to Nashville for a week-long convention of retired ministers? Naturally, when I heard about your terrible predicament, I packed up and left on the next plane out of Tampa. Flew in the middle of the night to get here this early, you know. That's what a good mother does." She sighed loud and long. Martyrdom did not look good on her.

And didn't that just add joy to my world? "No, Momma, you didn't mention Daddy's trip. I wish you had talked to me before you decided to come." I set a half-empty container of colored marshmallow Happy Critters and an unopened bag of generic bran flakes on the table. "I could have explained things over the phone and saved you the expense of your long trip." Saved us this awkward situation, too.

I jammed bread into the toaster and overfilled four mismatched glasses with no-pulp orange juice.

"Oh, no juice for me, dear," Momma said, waving her hand so I couldn't miss the new costume jewelry she sported. "The sugar content, you know. Bad for belly fat. I'll give you some diet tips while I'm here. I've joined a group of women at our park who know all about health foods. Staying in shape is so important." Her gaze narrowed. "I could even help you get rid of that little roll around your waist."

"Excuse me! The subject of my waistline is not up for discussion." *Especially in front of my daughter.* I snagged a handful of paper towels from the roll on the counter and started mopping up the spilled juice.

"My goodness, you're a bit testy in the morning, aren't you, dear? You should try a healthy smoothie to begin your day. You'd feel much better and lose a few pounds, too."

I pretended not to hear her. I finished wiping up the OJ mess, tossed the wad of paper towels in the trash, and grabbed a bowl. After pouring Happy Critters in it, I handed it to Betsy. "Sweetie, eat your breakfast. We're running late. So as soon as you're finished, brush your teeth and grab your books." I filled the other plates and offered one to Momma.

As I expected, she shook her head. "Oh, nothing for me. I usually have a fruit and yogurt smoothie. Frances Louise, you really must start watching your diet more closely." She dabbed her mouth, using the paper napkin like it was fine linen. I don't know why. She hadn't eaten a darn thing.

I opened my mouth to ask her if she'd forgotten Poppy Rose's death, but she cut me off with a wave of her hand. I wondered if God was testing me.

"I'm only concerned about you, Frances Louise."

"Momma, I know you didn't come all the way here to discuss my diet." Betsy was quietly taking it all in. "Hurry up and get your teeth brushed, sweetie. And change that blouse, too. You wore it yesterday."

Betsy left the room without protesting, albeit reluctantly. I didn't want her hearing any more of Momma's comments about my diet or Poppy's murder. I gave Momma my full attention. "I know Miss Nettie phoned you about what happened at the church."

Momma flinched but quickly recovered her composure. "Yes, she did, and that's why I'm here. To get the mess straightened out for you. It's not like we haven't been through this in the past."

That last comment punched my defensive button. This time, I knew I'd done nothing wrong.

"Stop beating around the bush, Momma. Just ask. Do you really think I murdered Poppy Rose? Do you?" Unexpected heat built up inside my chest, something that hadn't happened since I'd left home in disgrace. I could feel my cheeks burn. *Stop it, Frankie Lou! You're grown up now.*

Turning away from Momma's disapproving gaze, I took a calming breath. *I swear one more of her tsk-tsks and I'll . . .* Pesky tears stung my eyes, and I swiped them away with the back of my hand. Why do I let her do that?

Momma's concern, cloaked in not-so-subtle criticism, had always made me feel like a huge disappointment as a daughter. I guess some things never change. I returned to the table to gather up the last of the dirty dishes.

Instead of handing me my near-empty cup, Miss Nettie topped it off. "Let the dishes go and sit down, Frankie Lou. You've got enough time to finish your coffee."

Momma gave me that martyred parent look I hadn't seen since childhood. "Well, Frankie Lou may have time, but I've got things to do. I'd just like to know what happened."

Miss Nettie waited breathlessly for more gossip. The women were primed and ready with more questions. Outnumbered and knowing it, I pulled out my chair and sat.

Repeating my nighttime adventure to Momma while Miss Nettie made sure I didn't leave anything out that I'd already told her turned into a real challenge. I figured I deserved a medal of some sort. Both women insisted on talking at the same time and ended up sounding like presidential candidates during an election debate—talking a lot without saying anything worthwhile.

Two minutes into my explanation about the meeting and finding Poppy Rose in the baptistery, Miss Nettie was itching to run right out and play detective. Her sleuthing suggestions were straight out of TV's old *Magnum, P.I.* shows. That was so *not* happening. This was Texas, not Hawaii!

Momma declared I was giving her and Daddy a bad reputation again. Yeah, like that was my goal in life. Not!

"Momma, I'm the only witness the police have right now. Of course they suspect me. They suspect everyone who was at the deacons' meeting. They're questioning all of them."

I nibbled the last bit of sticky bun and took my sweet time chewing. Keeping my own investigative plans secret until I figured out who the most likely suspects were would require creativity and sneaky maneuvers on my part. But first, I had to actually have some plans in place before I could even have maneuvers. I'd have to be extremely careful or Momma and Miss Nettie would be bird-dogging my every move.

"The police have lots more people to question, but even though the circumstances make me a possible person of interest, I'm not worried, Momma. I'm innocent of any crime." I sounded way more confident than I felt, but I couldn't let down my guard. "I can handle the situation just fine."

Right then, Miss Nettie burst from her chair like a bottle rocket, startling Momma and me. "Frankie Lou, you get ready for work. Your momma can visit with me while I clear the table and do up the dishes." Her eyes narrowed in a *don't argue with me* look. "By the way, Louisa," she said to Momma as she gathered dirty dishes and carried them to the sink, "you didn't say how long you're planning to stay in town. Will the Reverend be joining you soon?"

Momma shook her head. Not a hair of her product-glossy, waved and sprayed "do" dared to move an inch. "No, Frank will be at the conference in Nashville for ten days. I've decided to stay right here with Frankie Lou and Betsy until school's out. Then Betsy will go home with me for the rest of the summer. I simply couldn't bear the thought of Frankie Lou letting that precious child fly all the way to Florida by herself. Why, I'd worry the entire time she was up in the air," she said. "She will be much safer flying back with me."

Pfftt! I'm not so sure about that. "Momma, letting Betsy fly down alone was your idea," I reminded her as politely as I could manage. *Lord, this wasn't what I had in mind when I asked for help. Surely, there's another option. Please?*

I wasn't done arguing. "School isn't out for another week. Then Betsy's going to church camp for two weeks. If she goes to Florida at all, it won't be until after the first of July, maybe later. Don't you remember? We made those plans earlier? Why would you think I'd change them now?"

Dear Lord, I love my momma but there is no way I can deal with her under my roof for more than a week. Amen.

Momma looked at me like God had given me a brain the size of a peach pit. "Why, the plans have to be changed now that you're in trouble again," she said as if she was talking to a kindergartner. Then she excused herself and left the room.

I hate when she talks down to me, but maybe she was right. Maybe I should think about canceling Betsy's camp trip and the visit to Florida until the problem here was solved. After all, I was still a person of interest in the homicide. I had to consider Betsy's safety first. Would she be safer at home or would I put her in jeopardy by keeping her with me? Holding my temper in check, I called after Momma. "Bathroom's down the hall." I figured that's where she was headed. My logical assumption couldn't have been more wrong. But then, Momma and logic were not close acquaintances.

Betsy stood the kitchen doorway, mouth quivering as she listened to her summer plans change without anyone even asking if she cared. The minute her Grammy was out of sight, she pulled a long face.

"Please, Momma, can't you tell Grammy I want to go to church camp with the rest of the kids in my Sunday school class? I don't want to be left out. We're taking a big bus, and it'll be so much fun." Tears shimmered in the corners of her summer-blue eyes. "I can still go, can't I, Momma? Please?"

I wanted to hold her and reassure her things would be okay, but I had to be careful not to treat her like a baby. My daughter depended on me to make everything in her world safe and happy, but she'd already begun to test her adolescent independence a little. The way things were going lately, I sure wasn't making any high marks in the "perfect mom" department. I settled for brushing a kiss across her cheek. I had no idea how to fix the ache in my heart. Finding Poppy's murderer might be a whole lot easier.

"Yes, sweetheart, I promise you'll go to church camp. Grammy won't be staying here very long." *Not if I can help it.*

Miss Nettie looked up at the sound of some loud thumping and scraping on the front porch about the same time as Betsy and I did. All three of us stared open-mouthed as Momma lugged two suitcases the size of steamer trunks through the front door, banging a dent in the door frame, taking paint off in the process. I wondered how much the airlines had charged her to check those big suckers.

Momma stopped directly in front of us and dropped the luggage, the heaviest one barely missing my foot. Hands on her hips, she addressed me in a cool, detached tone, much different than the one I listened to growing up.

"Which bedroom will be mine, dear? I'd like to get unpacked and settled in."

"There's only one bedroom, Momma. The one with the twin beds Betsy and I use."

Momma eyed my couch, dismissing it with a wave of her hand.

"Well, I could never sleep on one of those things. My back, you know. You're young and lucky you don't have such problems. Don't worry. I'm sure I'll be quite comfy in your bed, Frances Louise." She started down the hall. "Betsy, come help Grammy get settled, darling. We'll have such fun sharing your room."

Betsy's face crumpled. "I don't want to go to school today, Grammy. I don't feel so good."

Momma spun around in mid-step. "School? Isn't her school out for the summer now?" She was already checking Betsy's forehead for fever.

"Of course not, Momma. I told you she has another week of classes." With all the chaos and shock of yesterday's sad events, plus Momma's unexpected arrival this morning, it's a wonder I remembered my name. I definitely did not remember offering Momma my bed.

I hustled Betsy off to find her backpack for school. Then I grabbed Momma's luggage, pushing and shoving the cumbersome pieces all the way into my bedroom. While she unpacked, I quickly cleared a place for her in our messy closet.

"If you need anything else, just holler," I said, handing her some empty hangers. "I'll put fresh towels in the bathroom before I leave for work so you can freshen up."

Before she could fire another round of questions at me, I hurried back to the kitchen for one more bite of my cinnamon roll. I figured I deserved a treat after surviving the worst of the day's drama, namely Momma.

Leaning against the counter, I gave the room one final inspection. Bright and cheery, my tiny, red, white and gray kitchen was the first room I'd decorated when I moved in. With two buckets of paint, some peppermint-striped fabric, and a few decorative knick-knacks from the Goodwill store, I'd tackled the job with more determination than expertise. The result was a satisfying sense of pride.

Miss Nettie had put the last of the breakfast dishes away in the white-painted cupboards and swept the floor while I settled Momma in my bedroom and made a hurried effort to make myself presentable for work.

"What would I do without you, Miss Nettie?" I pushed away from the counter and held out my arms.

She reached out and welcomed my hug. "Pshaw! I'll be finished here in a jiffy. Go along now. Betsy's waiting for you to walk her to school and your momma's busy making herself at home in your bedroom. Go! Scoot!"

"Miss Nettie, I just plain love you. Thanks."

For the first time since I'd gotten out of bed that morning, I looked forward to leaving my little home. The prospect of having Momma underfoot for an undetermined length of time gave me severe heartburn. Her interference added enough extra agitation to turn that heartburn into Ulcer Central. I desperately wanted to run away from home, but couldn't.

"Honey, listen to me," Miss Nettie said, untying her apron and hanging it over the back of her chair. "You go on and send Betsy to that camp just like you planned. Don't worry about your momma. I'll find a way to keep her out of your hair while she's here." She patted my hand and winked. "Trust me. In a day or two she'll be mighty happy to head back to Florida."

Sighing, I shook my head. "I wish. But you know how Momma likes to be in the middle of everything. I don't need her reorganizing my life or criticizing my plans for the singers or the costumes."

For the kind of musical production I had in mind, I was pretty sure Momma would have plenty to say, none of it complimentary. I took one last bite of cinnamon roll. Sugar might not solve my problem, but it was better than dwelling on Momma's possible reaction to The Joyful Noise and whatever cockamamie notion she might have to stick her nose into the police investigation of Poppy Rose's death.

By the time I'd finished making my sweet tooth deliriously happy Miss Nettie had finished spiffing up my kitchen and gone home to feed Moses. That left me to deal with Momma. Out of desperation and a surge of stubbornness, I made a decision. If my parent intended to inhabit my space for the next week it was time to set down some house rules. My house—my rules, right?

"I'm leaving to take Betsy to school and go on to work, Momma," I called down the hall. "I'll be home a little after five. Why don't you spend the day visiting some of your friends?" I might as well have been talking to the wind.

Momma's head popped out from the bedroom doorway. "Oh, I have plenty to keep me busy, Frances Louise. After I finish tidying up your house and planning a nice, healthy meal for this evening, I intend to talk with Chief Jackson. When I pick up Betsy after school we'll go grocery shopping for a few items so I can give her a lesson in cooking healthy. Don't worry. I'll take care of everything."

Dear Lord, that's what I'm afraid of.

Chapter Eight

I gave up my one-sided argument with Momma and hurried Betsy out of the house. While we ran the last two blocks to Ruby Springs Elementary, I dodged her questions about last night with one of those *I-do-not-have-time-now-I-promise-we'll-talk-later* phrases moms are allowed to use in emergencies. Talking was barely possible between my huffing and puffing, anyway. Clearly, exercise needed to be added to my overloaded to-do list. And that would happen when the Rio Grande had icebergs and Momma stopped calling me Frances Louise.

When we reached the school campus, Betsy broke away to join some of the students milling about the schoolyard, laughing and delaying the inevitable until the last bell sounded. As I turned to leave, the words *police* and *body* reached my ears and I spun around to see who had spoken. Three mothers broke away from a knot of parents who were whispering and not-so-subtly pointing toward me. The trio quickly pulled their children away from Betsy and rushed them inside the building. What was that all about?

Another mother left the group and approached me. As she drew near, I noticed a touch of silver in her hair that made her appear a bit older than the other, much younger, women. Probably the grandparent of one of the students, not the parent, I reasoned.

"Hi, I'm Bella Dorsey, the owner of Bella's Books and Candles over on the corner of Sunnyside and Main," she said in a pleasantly soft voice. "You're a suspect in the death of Poppy Rose Fremont, right? Have the police made any more arrests?"

The woman's straightforward approach had me wondering if I was about to be judged on the spot. Not wanting to make myself appear guilty by acting defensive, I smiled and politely attempted to set the record straight. "No arrests have been made at all, as far as I know, Miz Dorsey. Why do you ask?"

She glanced in the direction of the group she'd just left, then leaned in closer and lowered her voice. "I thought you should know about a possible situation that might arise concerning you and your daughter, Miz McMasters."

Before she could explain further, the vibrant chatter of young voices across the school campus suddenly escalated to a noisy rumble of discord between insistent parents and students.

By now the three mothers who pulled their children away from Betsy had been joined by two more. Soon all the students had been sent inside by their parents and Betsy stood alone. She came to me with such a puzzled look on her face, my Momma Lion persona growled at the nerve of those women. How dare they?

"Better head for class, sweetie," I told her with a hug. "Remember, Grammy is picking you up this afternoon after school."

She waved and went inside, her backpack swaying. I turned my attention back to the woman standing next to me, an apologetic look on her face.

"I'm sorry that happened. After hearing about the unfortunate incident at Faith Community, it seems a few of the mothers have chosen not to allow their children to associate with your daughter. Something about subjecting their youngsters to a possibly undesirable friendship that could connect them with a murderer."

"But my daughter wasn't involved," I said.

Bella shook her head. "I certainly don't agree with their decision and told them so, but I thought you deserved a heads-up. It may not amount to anything, since I believe kids are smarter about picking their own friends if we guide quietly from the sidelines, but it doesn't hurt to be forewarned. I know most of those moms, and as a whole they're not a bad bunch, just young and inexperienced. And too quick to judge others."

I was beginning to like Bella Dorsey, one of the people I hadn't met since my return. "That certainly explains why Betsy got the cold shoulder treatment just now," I said. "I appreciate the warning." I offered my hand. "Please call me Frankie Lou."

Bella's smile widened as she shook my hand. "And I'd like it very much if you'd call me Bella. I understand you lived here until a few years ago. I've been here two years, so I don't know everyone yet. I'd be delighted if you'd stop by my shop sometime and look around. If you don't care for books, I also carry some lovely, one-of-a-kind handmade candles, and I'm considering adding a little coffee shop area next year." She checked her watch and gasped. "Oh, I really must run. I walk my grandson to school every day before I open the shop, and if I don't hurry, I'll be late. Bye now."

"Nice to meet you, Bella," I called after her and waved. She waved back when she reached the other side of the street, and I made a mental note to stop by her shop after all the uproar concerning Poppy's death was over and the murderer was behind bars. Until then, my days would be busy proving my innocence and working with The Joyful Noise singers.

I BURST THROUGH the door of the clinic two minutes late, not surprised to find my employer waiting for his morning coffee and watching the clock.

"Sorry, Doc. I would've been on time, but you won't believe what's been going on at my house."

Breathless from my race against time, I dropped my shoulder bag into the bottom drawer of my desk and set about filling the coffeemaker with water and measuring out coffee.

Doc waited until I'd turned on the unit before he spoke.

"Well?" Doc Adderly was a man of few words most of the time. A spry widower in his early seventies, he ran his animal clinic with a mixture of forty-plus years of experience in his field and down-home common sense. That combination, along with his no-nonsense work ethic, made his clinic one of Ruby Springs's most successful businesses. I was indebted to him for taking a chance when he hired me. I had no credentials except a healthy respect for animals, and I knew nothing about their medical care. Fortunately, I wasn't hired to cure their ills, and I'm a quick learner, so Doc put me in charge of keeping his office running smoothly. I loved everything about my job.

I pulled two mugs from an overhead cabinet and pretended I didn't hear him. He didn't fool me. The wily doctor never missed *The Early Reporter* morning news.

When I turned around, he shook his finger at me like a scolding parent. "I know you heard me, young lady. Now spill it. Is that nonsense I heard on the news true? Were you arrested for the murder of Poppy Rose?"

"No, Doc, cross my heart I wasn't arrested, but because I was the one who found Poppy Rose they took me to the police station for questioning. In the eyes of the town gossips, I guess that makes me guilty. I'm sure the coffee shop is buzzing by now."

"Hmmm." Doc rubbed his chin, studying me for so long I thought he'd zoned out. In a raspy voice caused by years of smoking, he asked, "Who questioned you, the chief or Detective Hardy?"

The coffee finished brewing, and I filled the mugs, handing one to him. He blew on the steaming liquid before taking a cautious sip.

"Both," I said and took a hit of caffeine. Today I needed all I could get. "To tell the truth, Doc, I don't think either one of them believed my story. And just when I thought things couldn't get any worse, Miss Nettie told me she called Momma last night. I thought she was joking until Momma showed up bright and early at my house this morning, ready to take on the entire Ruby Springs Police Department."

Coffee spewed from Doc Adderly's mouth like the fountain in the middle of the town square. I snagged a tissue from the box on my desk and handed it to him.

"You say your momma's in town?" he asked, wiping his chin and patting the front of his lab coat. His hand lingered on the chest pocket where, until a year ago, a pack of smokes had permanently resided. I know this because he'd made it quite clear during my initial job interview there'd be no smoking on the premises. Fine with me. In my opinion the habit was stinky as well as a health hazard.

"Oh, she's here, all right," I said. "Took a non-stop, red-eye flight out of Tampa, rented a car when she arrived at DFW, and was knocking on my door before breakfast with enough luggage for a month's stay. She's only been here a few hours and is already reorganizing my life."

I pulled out the desk chair, sat down, and rubbed my temples. A pesky headache blossomed inside my skull, the perfect follow-up to my day's already disastrous beginning. Hoping Doc would take the hint and leave so I could finish my paperwork, I opened the appointment book and began to check it against a stack of notes by the phone. My job was beginning to depend on sticky notes.

Doc didn't budge, just looked at me over the rim of his cup, his eyebrows wiggling like a pair of wooly caterpillars.

"Once your momma catches the video on the TV news report, I'll bet dollars to doughnuts she won't be going back to Florida any time soon."

"Don't even think such thoughts, Doc," I said, keeping my head down as I logged in tomorrow's scheduled appointments.

"Well, that video clearly showed a cop taking you inside the church when the EMTs rolled the gurney outside and the latest news flash this morning identified the victim as Poppy Rose. Doesn't take much imagination to figure out what was going on. Your momma's no dummy, kiddo."

If the news video had given Doc the wrong impression and Poppy'd been identified, I had to set him straight. No telling how many times his clients would ask about me. He needed to know the truth, but I had orders from the chief and Detective Hardy to keep quiet until an official report came from police headquarters. Doc's support would be important if I remained a suspect in the eyes of the law. Resigned to the fact he wasn't dropping the subject until he had some answers, I closed the appointment book and settled back to fill him in on as much as I was at liberty to tell. At least I didn't have to keep Poppy's identity a secret any longer.

I'd barely gotten started relating last night's events when the bell over the clinic door clanged the arrival of the day's first client. Relieved to have our conversation delayed, I registered Fanny Teasdale's three-legged cat for its regular check-up.

"I'll expect more details at the next break between patients, you hear?" With that, he shuffled off to the examining room.

The morning flew by without a break. Walk-ins, as well as scheduled appointments, made it impossible for us to continue our conversation until noon. I was happy to have something besides the investigation to think about. Unfortunately for me, I underestimated the local pet owners' interest in Poppy's demise since she'd been identified as the victim by the media.

Every time a walk-in arrived at the clinic with an animal they wanted Doc to examine, the first question they asked me was how Poppy Rose looked when I found her in the baptistery. My answer was the same to everyone. "Dead. Wet and dead." What did they expect?

Okay, so I didn't make any effort to sound respectful but hey, what was wrong with these people? Two out of three nosy female clients eyed me up and down like I'd already been convicted. They didn't deserve a straight answer any more than I deserved their biased opinions.

One rather exotic-looking young woman didn't even bother to bring an animal with her. She'd stopped in for only one reason—to ask some mighty personal questions about Ruby Springs's unmarried chief of police. Uh, yeah, like I'd share that kind of gossip even if I had it.

Another cat owner actually forgot why she'd brought her pet in to see the doctor. But the most upset client of the day was poor Wilbur Hadley. When he brought in his high-strung Siamese cat they both looked like candidates for a heavy-duty tranquilizer.

"How can doc help you this morning, Mr. Hadley?"

Right out of the blue he said, "They questioned me, too. I didn't know anything about the faucet or how Poppy got in the baptistery. Why did they question me? I didn't kill her."

His sudden outburst caught me by surprise. I hadn't even mentioned the incident. "Don't worry, Mr. Hadley. You weren't the only one questioned. The police talked with everyone who attended the meeting. Just routine, that's all." I spoke softly so as not to agitate him more. The man was nervous as a streetwalker at a tent revival. "Why don't you sit down and catch your breath? I'll bring you a glass of water."

"No water, thank you, Frankie Lou. But I will sit down. You know this whole thing is tragic, simply tragic. And to think it's been left up to me to make the funeral arrangements. Extremely upsetting. I thought Poppy's—I mean, Miz Fremont's family would take care of all that."

He took a seat on the bench in front of the window to wait. The Siamese twitched its tail and meowed loudly, watching me with evil-looking eyes. I expected the creature to pounce on me at any moment.

"I'm sorry you have to deal with the sad details," I said, wondering why the job had fallen on his stooped shoulders. Poor man looked ready to keel over with fright. I checked the appointment book but didn't find his name. Odd. "By the way, Mr. Hadley, what time was your appointment today? I must've forgotten to write it down."

"Oh, I don't have an appointment," he said. "I just stopped in to offer you my condolences."

I must've looked puzzled because he stammered his explanation. "For, uh, your arrest last night."

Another misconception thanks to the local media. "Not arrested, Mr. Hadley, just questioned like everyone else."

He looked confused for a minute, which made two of us. Then he got up and left without another word.

As I watched him go, the disturbing realization that even after death, Poppy Rose still managed to keep the local gossip hotline busy made me want to chew nails. Bless her heart.

My concentration wasn't worth two cents after lunch, either. Images of last night's bizarre tragedy stayed trapped in my mind like a fly in a spider's web. To keep me totally discombobulated mentally, a vision of Joe Camps's face got all tangled up in my thoughts, and that was just wrong. Thankfully I managed to focus on the work in front of me with a minimum of errors.

The surge of local pet owners lining up to see Doc Adderly kept me busy filling out admission forms. Every four-legged critter in Ruby Springs suddenly needed medical attention. Still, the patients provided a diversion I welcomed, and I managed to shake the worrisome thoughts about Poppy's attack from my mind. Unfortunately, Joe Camps's image was determined to stay.

Doc scurried back and forth checking patients, his white lab coat flapping every which way. Since most of the pets weren't really sick and their owners were only there for the gossip, Doc's per-patient time was cut in half. That doubled the day's income and put a smile on the old boy's face. *Cha-ching!* He sure did love days like this.

After a quick attempt to eat my peanut butter and grape jelly sandwich during our unusual noon rush, I was in the infirmary holding a sad-faced Schnauzer puppy while Doc administered the little guy's first shots. Even as soft-hearted as I am, helping out like this when Doc asked didn't bother me. The inoculations were for the puppy's health and safety. Besides, I don't ever look at the needle.

After the procedure I took the trembling puppy to his owner in the waiting room and returned to the treatment room, still puzzling over Poppy's funeral arrangements.

There was something odd about Deacon Hadley making the arrangements for Poppy's funeral service. Not my responsibility, I reminded myself. But if the police notified Poppy Rose's parents, Poke and Pearlene deHaven, wherever they were, wouldn't they want to decide how their only daughter would be buried? I hoped the divorced pair wouldn't make a scene if they decided to show up. No matter how I felt about her, Poppy deserved a little respect at her funeral.

"Do you know if the funeral's been scheduled yet, Doc?"

Doc had already put his instruments away and was washing up at the stainless steel sink. He stood with his back to me, but his answer was loud and clear over the running water.

"Well, I saw Marv Reedy from the funeral home at the coffee shop this morning. He said maybe another week. Wasn't positive, though."

"That long? Did he say why?" I started washing up at the sink across the room. We were still back to back as we talked.

"Guess the investigation's taking longer than expected. Chief Jackson refuses to release the body. Wilbur Hadley's in charge of the funeral arrangements. I think Poke called him from Padre Island about taking care of them." Doc finished scrubbing and came to stand beside me. "How many more patients we got left, Frankie Lou? I could sure use a cup of coffee about now to go with those fried pies I snagged from the coffee shop this morning."

"The Schnauzer was the last one scheduled. We're finished unless we get another walk-in." I pulled a paper towel from the wall dispenser and dried my hands.

"Good. How about putting on a fresh pot while I warm up the fried pies?"

"Sure thing, Doc." *Fried pies, oh boy!* Grinning, I hurried to the front office and got busy. I even managed to complete the last of the day's paperwork while the coffee brewed.

Doc returned a few minutes later with the pies on a paper plate, all warm and gooey right out of the microwave, and set them, along with two plastic forks, on the desk top. I got up to pour the coffee. Heaving a deep sigh, he sank down in the worn leather chair behind my desk.

"Frankie Lou, I swear I don't know how I got along before you came to work for me. The number of patients has doubled in the last couple of months. Not that I'm complaining. I just don't understand where they're all coming from. I'm beginning to feel every one of my so-called golden years."

He raised his cup of coffee to his lips and blew on it before tasting. Nothing fancy about Doc. No, sir!

I could hardly wait to ask more questions about the funeral and to find out more about Poppy's family, but the aroma of the warm pies was too tempting to ignore. I leaned against the side of my desk, and I picked up my pie with my fingers and took a bite.

"Mmmm, peach. Oh lordy, I've died and gone to Heaven." I moaned in pie ecstasy around a mouth full of the luscious pastry. "My favorite." Any questions I had could wait but not for long.

We ate in silence, savoring the pies like they were the last meal we'd have in this life. I finished mine ahead of Doc, licked the sticky sweetness from my fingers, and poured another cup of coffee.

Doc put his hand over his cup. "No more for me, thanks. Too much caffeine makes me shaky. Not good in this profession. Besides, you know I like my brew lukewarm."

I remembered, all right. I set the coffee pot back in place and turned off the brewer, questions about Poppy's family stuck in my mind like the duct tape that had been wrapped around poor Poppy.

"So why don't you go ahead and ask me, Frankie Lou? I can tell you're dying to know if Poke and Pearlene are coming to the service, aren't you?"

I laughed. "How do you do that, Doc? Are you a psychic?"

"Nope, but you'll never make a poker player, young lady. Your face is as easy to read as a first-grade primer." He picked up his cup, drank the coffee cooled now the way he liked it.

"Well, are they?" I couldn't wait any longer to ask, imagining the chaos that would erupt when those two arrived.

Doc nodded. "Marv said the detective was the one who contacted them. Poke told him he'd call Wilbur to handle the details. You know Poke's down on Padre Island with his new lady friend. Can't remember her name. I don't know if they're married or not."

I put the last crumb of pie in my mouth. "What connection does Wilbur have with Poppy Rose? Or Poke, for that matter?"

"Oh, Wilbur's the Fremont financial advisor. At least, that's what he calls himself. I'm not so sure if that's his legal title. Parvis hired him as his accountant right after he and Poppy Rose got married. She's supposedly the one who gave him the uppity title of financial advisor. Don't think he's connected to Poke except through Parvis." Doc put his hands behind his head, cocked it to one side like he was doing some deep thinking and stretched. Today's full and often frantic schedule had exhausted him.

"That doesn't explain why Poke or Pearlene wouldn't want to handle the funeral details. After all, Poppy was their daughter." I felt guilty asking more questions but I wanted to hear about the deHavens and the Fremonts. Miss Nettie had been unusually vague on that particular topic of interest.

Doc eyed me straight on. "How long have you been gone from Ruby Springs, Frankie Lou?"

When he had a mind to, Doc could side-step questions slicker than a crooked lawyer. I laughed. This was one of those times.

"Have you forgotten what happened right after I graduated, Doc? My parents nearly had side by side heart attacks when B.J. and I had to get married. Remember how we left town right after the wedding? Momma accused us of causing the biggest scandal in the history of Ruby Springs. Daddy made it clear I'd shamed them. I was scared to leave with B.J., being pregnant and all, but wasn't about to stay."

Doc rubbed his chin like he always did when he was pondering. "No, child, I didn't forget any of that commotion, or how sorry I was that your folks didn't stand by you. However, the biggest shock was the fact your daddy even owned a shotgun. Your wedding barely made second on the gossip chart." He chuckled then, and I knew he was remembering that day. "After the talk about you and B.J. died down, the town stayed pretty quiet. Then Poppy Rose got herself engaged to Parvis Fremont a few years ago, and that scandal dang near sent the town into a gossiping frenzy. No one knew anything about Parvis except he was older than her daddy and had a heap of money. Fanciest wedding ever held in Ruby Springs. Biggest waste of money there ever was. Doves don't belong at weddings. Least ways inside the church. Messy, doncha' know?"

He paused like he was searching his memory for archived information before he continued. "Wilbur Hadley came to town about . . . oh, mebbe four or five years before Parvis and Poppy Rose married and moved into that big custom-built mansion of theirs. Don't know why two people needed such a big house." Doc scratched his head.

"So Wilbur didn't know Parvis before the wedding, just Poppy Rose?"

"That's right. Wilbur's a clerk in Foster Gates's office downtown and does tax returns on the side in his home. Gates is the attorney who handled Parvis's estate. That's how Wilbur met Parvis. I heard he took over the financials after Parvis died, but Gates remained executor. Wilbur and the Fremonts weren't close friends. Just happened to be members of the same church. Didn't socialize with the same circle of friends, though. Guess that doesn't matter now with both the Fremonts gone, does it?"

"No, I guess it doesn't," I answered.

Doc stood up, yawned and said, "Let's lock up for the day, kiddo. I'm plumb tuckered out." With a two-finger salute he left the room.

I gathered up the daily work sheets to be filed the next morning and straightened my desk. The day had been busier than usual, and I was ready to go home, too, but having a neat work area when I come in each morning makes a better start to my day. I flipped over the CLOSED sign on the door and went back to my desk to make some last minute notes.

I had my head down concentrating on writing myself a note to call the supplier tomorrow for more antiseptic solution when the loud clang of the brass bell on the door made me jump up so fast my shin whacked the sharp corner of the desk. Darn it! I'd forgotten to turn the lock when I'd turned the sign over. Couldn't people read?

Chapter Nine

Hobbling toward the door, I got there just as a woman burst into the room on a blast of hot, late afternoon air. She held an injured dog away from her body like it was a furry bomb fixin' to explode.

"Someone take this nasty thing." Her shrill voice pierced my eardrums and no doubt those of everyone else within a three-mile radius.

Like the opening scene right out of an old Hollywood noir movie, the silver-blond Marilyn Monroe look-alike swept into the waiting room on a wave of designer perfume strong enough to make my eyes water. The glare from all the bling draped on her perfectly constructed body made me wish for sunglasses.

I blinked, held my finger under my nose to suppress a sneeze, and eyed the moaning animal in the woman's arms. The pooch wasn't big but definitely not one of those teensy, purse-sized dogs, either. In fact, I'd bet my brand-new, dangly earrings from the Dollar'n'Dime that Blondie here was experiencing an uncomfortable twinge of conscience for hitting the poor ditch-dog with her car. Accident or not, she could've shown a little compassion.

I'm not usually so quick to judge, but hey, her penciled and painted face had Drama Queen written all over it, and I'd already had a disastrous run-in with one of those types, God rest her soul. I'm pretty sure natural eyebrows aren't shaped like the St. Louis Arch, either. The thought that she and Poppy Rose must've patronized the same nip-and-tuck salon was a fleeting blip on my brain's radar screen. What the heck was going on in Ruby Springs, anyway? Had the whole town gone high-fashion crazy? First, Poppy Rose and now this Dixie Darlin'.

I lifted the whimpering pooch from the woman's arms, careful not to add to the dog's injuries, and assured her she'd come to the right place. "We'll take good care of him, ma'am. Don't you worry. Dr. Adderly's the best around."

"I don't care what you do with the disgusting thing. Just take it."

Gosh, lady, tell me how you really feel. "Doc will take a look at him right away."

Ms. Wanna-Be-Marilyn spied the hand cleaner dispenser on the counter and pumped half-a-dozen frantic squirts into her bejeweled hands, scrubbing them like she was fixing to perform surgery. I expected her to shower with it any minute now.

"Front and center, Doc! Emergency!" My shout brought Doc Adderly hustling from the treatment area at the rear of the clinic, his kindly face full of concern for the injured animal, though not so much for the blond. Did I mention he's nearing seventy? I think maybe his priorities have shifted a bit, if you get my drift. He didn't even give the woman his usual friendly Texas "Hey, how're y'all today?"

"Bring the patient on back, Frankie Lou, so I can take a look." He jerked his thumb toward the back room but kept an eye on the blond. Okay, so I was wrong. How could he not notice blatant bling overkill?

When the woman turned to leave, Doc's hand shot up like a traffic cop's, instantly squashing her plan. "Ma'am, before you leave there's papers you need to fill out. I'll let you know what I find after I examine your dog. Meantime, have a seat."

Since I had my hands full of the trembling patient, Doc grabbed a clipboard with two printed forms from my desk, tucked a pen inside the clip, and shoved them at her. Then, white lab coat flapping, he whirled off to do his job.

Her vermillion mouth agape, which, I might add looked like collagen overkill, she stomped a stiletto-clad foot, her rapid words firing like bullets. "It's not my dog and I don't have time to fill out any stupid papers. Just take the horrid thing so I can leave."

Well, now, I've seen bad manners before, but this prima donna took the prize. Doc's neck got redder by the minute as he strode out of the room. He wasn't one to cotton to rudeness, no matter who the smart-ass was. Oops, sorry. My description, not Doc's, and I apologize for that. Sometimes my vocabulary slips a bit. I'm trying real hard to not trip up too often, especially around my daughter.

"We need the information for our files, ma'am. Please fill it out like the doctor asked. And help yourself to some coffee." I nodded toward the half-full coffee pot on top of the file cabinet and the stack of foam cups beside it. "I'll be back as soon as Doc finishes with his evaluation."

The woman gave a derisive snort, so I focused my attention on the trembling pooch and scooted through the examining room door. Thank goodness Betsy hadn't come here after school today to witness the woman's lack of manners. Drama Queen was definitely not from around here, bless her heart.

The dog moaned when I laid him on the table. I stroked his head. "Poor old thing," I murmured. "You look like you haven't eaten for a week."

The mongrel's ribs stuck out like the picked-over carcass of a Thanksgiving turkey. Blood and dirt matted his scruffy coat. I didn't know how serious his injuries were, but the bad feeling hovering over the room was hard to ignore.

Nodding at me when I entered the room, Doc finished scrubbing his hands, snapped on gloves, and gently started the examination. The dog whimpered pathetically. I sniffled, holding back sympathetic tears every time the dog moaned. Good thing Doc appreciated my competence as his receptionist enough to overlook my tender heart in the treatment room.

The examination didn't take long. Doc looked at me with a big smile on his leathery face. "This is one lucky dog, Frankie Lou. Don't know what kind of vehicle smacked him, but there's nothing broken, just a couple of contusions on one hip and some minor cuts on his head. Only needs a few stitches. I want to keep him overnight for observation, though. He needs something to eat and a good night's rest."

He jerked his head toward the outer office. "You go on out there now and deal with that woman while I finish up here. And make sure she fills out those blasted forms. I don't care who she is or where she's from. Get her address and bill her just the same as anyone. Tell her she can pick up the dog in the morning."

I sighed. Some days it would be easier to be the doc and only have to deal with animals. The human species leave a lot to be desired when it comes to good behavior. I've learned that from working with both types.

"And find out what street she was driving on when she hit the dog. Might help us find the dog's owner," Doc called out as I started out of the room.

"Yes, sir," I said and headed up front, not eager to dispense the good doctor's orders. Finding the dog's real owner wouldn't be easy. Most likely the pooch was a stray. I fought against the word *adoption* sneaking into my head. I did NOT need a dog, especially one I'd already named Lucky in my mind.

The waiting room was strangely quiet when I walked in. "Ma'am?" My gaze searched the room, though I could clearly see it was empty. No answer. No Make-Believe-Marilyn.

I crossed the room and stepped outside just in time to see the back of a dark sedan burn rubber and speed away down the street.

"Hey, wait a minute! Come back here!" I shook my fist at the departing vehicle, but my shout was lost in the engine's roar. I clamped my mouth shut before another one of B.J.'s colorful phrases escaped. I really needed to work on refining that part of my vocabulary, but at the moment, I was royally pissed.

Thanks to the snooty blond who'd cleverly skipped without leaving her name, the clinic would have to absorb the cost of the dog's care. I know this fact because I'm also Doc's bookkeeper, in addition to acting as receptionist and sometime surgical assistant. This unexpected expense would pinch the clinic's monthly budget tighter than an old maid's corset. *And most likely my salary, too.*

Reluctantly, I headed to the back room to give Doc the bad news. I could hardly wait to see what other surprises the rest of the week held. After Poppy's death this oddly suspicious incident with a total stranger had me jumping at my own shadow.

I decided to call an impromptu meeting tonight to tell my young singers the only good news to come from last night's meeting. My attitude needed a boost. With my shoulders squared, I pushed open the door to the infirmary.

"Guess what, Doc?"

He gently moved the dog to a padded bed inside a large, wire holding cage before he answered.

"The fancy gal skipped out, eh?" He went to the sink, removed his gloves, and pumped a good-sized blob of antiseptic soap in the palm of one hand. "Not surprised," he said as he scrubbed his hands hard enough to take the skin off. "Not surprised at all." He kept on scrubbing another minute.

"What makes you say that, Doc? From the way she was dressed, she must've had plenty of money."

"Well," he drawled, pulling a paper towel out of the wall dispenser and working on his wet hands, "you haven't been here long enough to know this, Frankie Lou, but I usually get lots of walk-ins during the summer, mostly tourists who don't have sense enough to leave their pets at home while they're on vacation. Don't you go worrying too much over this one. We'll get by. Besides, a new client's bringing a puppy in for a check-up tomorrow. Initial exam and shots'll add a few dollars to the till." He winked, pulled out another paper towel, and finished drying his hands.

He was joking, of course. Doc wasn't the type to pad a patient's bill simply to cover a bad account, but this time I felt he'd be justified if he did.

"That woman could've paid the bill twice over with all the sparkly jewelry she was wearing," I said. "Biggest diamond ring I ever laid eyes on. Why do the rich ones always manage to get away with cheating?"

Doc got quiet for a minute, then with a solemn face said, "Sometimes they don't, child. Sometimes they don't."

For goodness sakes, what did that mean?

The hairs on the back of my neck prickled like someone had dosey-doe'd across my grave. I pinched my arm just hard enough to know I wasn't dead yet. Even so, something mighty strange was going on in Ruby Springs.

TRUE TO HER WORDS, Momma was building her version of a healthy dinner when I got home from work. The only items I recognized as she chopped and diced were the field greens, tofu, and almonds. I didn't dare ask what the rest of the ingredients in the big mixing bowl were. I'm not against eating healthy, mind you. I just like to know what I'm putting in my mouth and where it came from. Don't want any surprises when I bite into something expecting sweet and getting sour, thank you very much.

As soon as I saw what Momma was concocting, I took Betsy aside and explained that she wasn't to complain out loud about her Grammy's cooking. I whispered I'd already ordered pizza for the night's impromptu meeting with The Joyful Noise kids, so she was more than happy to agree. At our house, pizza is a big treat. Thank goodness for today's Two for One sale at Pizza Pleez.

Miss Nettie was bringing cookies and lemonade. She and I had agreed not to tell Momma about the meeting. The less my "let-me-tell-you-how-it-should-be-done" parent knew ahead of time, the less chance she'd have to try to control everything.

Just before dinner, Momma announced she and her long-time friend, Gladys Mears, were meeting at Mavis Benson's home for an evening of reminiscing—otherwise known as gossip. I could barely keep from jumping up and down. *Hallelujah! Thank you, Jesus.*

As soon as Momma left, Betsy tossed the tofu meal in the garbage while I got busy and whipped up grilled cheese sandwiches and tomato soup for anyone who didn't want pizza. Cheese for protein and tomato for Vitamin C. My kind of healthy.

Getting ready for the teens' arrival didn't take long. My only furniture in the living-slash-dining room of my little home was a well-used sofa bed and one equally well-used easy chair.

I dragged in the two dinette chairs from around the red vinyl-topped kitchen table, and Betsy grabbed the extra straight chair Miss Nettie loaned me after Momma showed up. That left plenty of empty floor space where the kids could sit.

There wasn't any actual rehearsing planned with the kids this evening. We hadn't even picked out songs for the contest yet. What I wanted to do was simply discuss my ideas with the group and get their opinions on some possible numbers for them to perform. After all, the whole point of establishing The Joyful Noise was to give them an outlet for their musical talent and boost their self-confidence. If I could show them how to have some fun while they rocked the community on its conservative heels, well, that would be extra hot sauce on my enchilada. Besides, I was counting on the teens to take my mind off the other, less happy events occurring in my life right now.

Betsy joined my hurried attempt at housekeeping by plumping a couple of oversized floor pillows I'd bought on sale. Tossed on the floor, they made colorful, soft seating. Kids'll sit anywhere, and I wasn't worried about impressing them.

What worried me, though, was whether or not my unfortunate confrontation with Poppy Rose would be misconstrued by the police. And if so, would my good intentions turn sour and make me liable for her death? I almost dreaded going back to the church annex next week. I had the strangest premonition that the police had missed an important clue that could help unravel the mystery—and whatever it was somehow involved the church.

By the time seven-thirty rolled around, I'd pushed my frettin' to the back corner of my mind and was eagerly waiting for the kids to arrive. They'd all made the trek over from the trailer park together. Everyone, that is, except Wesley. He and his dad strolled up the sidewalk a half-hour later.

I intended to ask Wesley why they hadn't joined the other kids on the walk to my house, but seeing Joe Camps when I opened the front door momentarily robbed me of my good sense. I invited him inside before I could stop myself. Go figure. He still "toted enough adorable" to be dangerous. Lordy! My reaction was the same as when I'd picked him up at the police headquarters—surprise and a racing heartbeat.

Warning bells clanged inside my head—a jarring reminder to back away from those bad boy types. Joe Camps was temptation and trouble with a capital T, just like my sexy ex had been. Even though I tried, I couldn't stop staring at his mouth when he spoke. Or the rolled up sleeves of his plain blue chambray work shirt, where biceps flexed when he moved, hinting of workouts during his time behind bars. Those muscles didn't get that way overnight. A slight shadow of dark whiskers defined a rugged jawline and added more hotness to the man than ought to be legal. But who's noticing?

"Oh, sorry, what did you say?" I stammered, staring into his chocolate-colored eyes.

He smiled. "No thanks, Miz McMasters. I'm on my way to check out a possible job. Thought I'd walk along with Wes since I was going this way. I'll take a rain check on the invite, though." His smile grew wider, teasing the corners of his mouth into a sexy curve. No fair! For a minute, I almost forgot where I was and why.

"Oh, well, of course," I said, forcing reality back in place. "Good luck on your job hunt." I don't know if I was relieved or disappointed by his refusal, but my sudden case of wandering stupids gave me a pretty good clue.

"Just call me Joe," he said, his words sliding out in a deep rumble, sending shivers through my body at lightning speed. Holy Moley! Sam Elliott? Yeah, that kind of voice.

"Come time any back, Joe. I mean, come back any time!" Sheesh! My words had the stupids, too.

He chuckled softly then, lifted his hand in a salute as he took off down the walk. Totally lacking any sign of sense, let alone appearing mature enough to mentor a room full of teenagers, I stumbled back inside only to be greeted by loud hoots and hollers from the three boys. The trio of giggling girls huddled together on the sofa whispering behind their hands. Kids!

"Way to go, Miz Frankie Lou." Bruno Brown rolled his eyes and gave me a thumbs-up. His devilish grin told me his male imagination was working overtime.

"Knock it off, you guys!" Wesley muttered, sinking back in the depths of the worn recliner, clearly embarrassed by the whole thing.

"Aw, you don't mind a little teasing do you, Miz Frankie Lou?" Bruno's grin was infectious. "We were just having a little fun."

When Bruno Brown spoke, everyone listened. I could see why the other kids followed his lead. He had the winning personality of a leader. Fun-loving but clearly respected within this tight little group of friends.

"No, I don't mind, Bruno," I lied, hoping my burning cheeks didn't give me away. "A little teasing is fine as long as no one gets hurt."

"We'd never let that happen, Miz Frankie Lou. Honest."

"I believe you." Despite his earlier rowdiness, Bruno was a good kid. In his own way, he was mentoring, too, and doing a darn good job of it. I could hardly wait to hear him vocalize.

"I see you've brought your own accompaniment." I pointed to the scratched guitar leaning against the side of the sofa. "Want to do a little jamming to get warmed up?"

The way they all started whooping and hollering you'd have thought I'd invited those kids to a Keith Urban or Blake Shelton concert. Personally, I'd choose George Strait. Bruno picked up his guitar, knocked off a few practice chords, and then those six young people surprised me by belting out a song they'd been rehearsing privately.

Talk about incredible, they were so amazing I wanted to shout "Dawg!" like Randy Jackson on American Idol. Even Miss Nettie, standing in the kitchen doorway, clapped her hands. Next to her, Betsy did her own preteen style of moving to the music.

I couldn't help laughing as their enthusiasm and energy surged through the room, chasing away the gloom and doom that had hovered over me all day. I couldn't let my worrisome personal situation keep me from making this unscheduled rehearsal a night these kids would always remember. Still, in spite of their eagerness, my anxiety hung on like the last sniffles of a bad cold.

There was only one problem with the group's choice of songs. *Moves Like Jagger* wasn't exactly gospel music. However, I had to admit their rendition did include some mighty impressive moves. I loved the way they got right into the spirit of the music.

"Wow! Y'all truly have been practicing," I said, impressed by their professional presentation. I reconsidered my thoughts about the song choice. That particular style of music would certainly appeal to the younger crowd. I was tempted to let them add a little fancy footwork to their first public appearance. A popular song would make a perfect hook to draw in the younger crowd and perhaps set the older generation tapping its toes.

I was mulling over all these new options when Bruno's younger brother, Granville, piped up. "If you don't like that song, Miz Frankie Lou, we've got us a couple more. Do you like country? The girls do a wicked version of Pistol Annie's *Hell on Heels*. Or we can rap for you, too."

Shoot. This singing gig was turning into a bigger challenge than I'd anticipated.

"Do you happen to know any gospel numbers?" I hadn't specifically asked them to practice those types of songs. In fact, I'd never mentioned what kind of music we'd be using. The looks on their faces told me I'd made a huge mistake.

Six pairs of eyes stared at me like I'd just asked them to sing *The Star Spangled Banner* in Latin. I held my breath.

After a thoughtful pause, Wesley raised his hand. "You mean like church songs, Miss Frankie Lou? Shoot, we thought we'd be singing fun songs. That's why we've been practicing popular stuff. That Jagger one was on the charts a long time 'n we already know all the words."

Fifteen-year-old J'Nell Franklin twirled a strand of white-blond hair around her finger and put her two cents worth into the conversation. "I wanted to do Lady GaGa's *Born This Way*, but Bruno said we didn't have enough time to learn all of it. We like songs with a beat. You know, snappy ones like Katy Perry's *Roar*, not those dull, preachy kinds." The look in her eyes dared me to question her choice.

Like Joy, her shy, fraternal twin, J'Nell was college level book-smart, but unlike Joy, she carried a huge, defensive chip on her shoulder and was as unpredictable as a riled up rattler when challenged by strangers. I was pretty sure I qualified as a stranger in her book right now.

Note to self: work on better communication with J'Nell. I understood how J'Nell felt. Her high IQ wouldn't do her any good if she didn't know how to fit comfortably into today's society. I didn't know much about the girls' home life, only that their single mom had two younger children besides the twins and was on welfare. No father in sight.

Again, I felt the frustration of these kids who'd been labeled *different*, but were simply misunderstood. Been there, done that, hated the darn tee shirt!

My original idea to organize a choral group was meant to give a boost of self-confidence to these kids. Watching them sing and dance tonight put a whole new slant on my plan. They were talented, natural-born musicians, and they loved singing. Why not put some gospel singing in a Broadway-style musical, instead of an ordinary choral concert where everyone wears dark choir robes and stands on stage like immovable statues? Talent like these kids totes deserved to be given a chance to shine.

My imagination took flight like a freed bird, and I let it soar, dazzled by ideas for fantastic costumes, stage sets, and Usher-like dance moves.

Why not? Realistically, I wasn't sure we could we pull it off without getting run out of town. I didn't want to make matters worse for these kids. After all, I still had my own reputation to redeem.

"Okay, I understand what you're saying." I put a CD in my portable player. "But, give a listen to this and tell me what you think." I held my breath and waited for the kids' reaction to the Statler Brothers version of *Will the Circle Be Unbroken.*

Bruno quickly picked up the melody on his guitar, Wesley harmonized, Granville drummed out the beat on the black enameled top of my wooden coffee table with a pair of battered drumsticks, and Joy and J'Nell added their soprano and alto harmony to the chorus. Their version wasn't perfect, but it was a start.

The biggest surprise of the evening was tiny Rosella Bird, a timid, seventeen-year-old with a powerful, Whitney Houston-like voice that knocked me six ways to Sunday when she sang *Amazing Grace.* Why on earth wasn't that incredible voice in the high school choir? In my opinion, every one of these kids could hold their own in tryouts for the school music department.

Happy tears stung my eyes when Miss Nettie gave an arthritic thumbs-up sign from the kitchen doorway.

Two hours and three large pizzas later, the enthusiastic jam session proved what I'd suspected all along. There was no limit to the talents of The Joyful Noise singers. This motley mix of friends was over-the-moon excited about competing for the Blue Ribbon at Ruby Springs's Community Summer Fest contest next month.

A little bit country, a little bit rock 'n' roll, and a whole lotta' gospel. Ruby Springs, here we come. Hallelujah! Amen, y'all!

After filling their stomachs with pizza and Miss Nettie's cookies and lemonade, the kids packed up their gear, and I waved them out the door. This time Wesley joined with them on their way back to the trailer park. I wondered how his dad's job search had turned out.

Miss Nettie was her usual efficient self, so with Betsy's help we hurried to put the house back in order before Momma returned from her ladies' night out.

I gave Miss Nettie a hug when she left and thanked her for everything. "Oh, I enjoyed it, my dear. I feel years younger when I'm around young folks. My, those kids tonight sure do know how to sing. I can't wait for them to walk off with a Blue Ribbon at the Summer Fest." She patted my arm. "Now, I must get home and let Moses out for a little while. And for goodness sakes, don't you worry a bit about your momma. I'll think of something to keep her out of your hair." She waved as she headed down the sidewalk.

"I know you will, Miss Nettie," I called after her. She said something back to me, but I couldn't hear her words clearly. Probably just thanking me. I nodded like I understood and went back inside to send Betsy off to bed with a kiss.

With only a few days left to get the singers ready to give a pre-contest audition for the deacons, and the mystery behind Poppy Rose's death still unsolved, my mind was flooded with disturbing thoughts. Hoping life would look better tomorrow after a good night's sleep, I headed for the bathroom to get ready for bed. Remembering I hadn't locked the front door, I turned around to take care of the chore when I heard a car honking loudly out front. I yanked open the door and stepped out on the porch. Ohmygosh! I'd completely forgotten about Momma!

She whipped her snappy, little rented convertible into the driveway and was out of the car and on the porch quicker than God could blink. "Wait, Frances Louise, don't lock up yet!"

For a woman wearing high-heeled sandals she was mighty agile. I marveled at the way she negotiated the steps. She dismissed me with an impatient wave of her hand and sashayed past right on into the kitchen. Uh-oh. Someone must've ruffled her feathers at the hen party.

I had to smooth those feathers like a dutiful daughter or suffer her constant fault-finding. I asked sweetly, "Did you have a good time with your friends, Momma?"

"Good time? *Humph!* I was humiliated. The main topic of conversation was my only daughter's police record and that video everyone in town has seen."

She took a pitcher from the fridge, poured a glass of the cucumber and lemon water she'd made this afternoon, and pointed to the chairs around my kitchen table. "Sit down, Frances Louise. We need to talk." I did as she asked and prepared for the worst.

"When I got to Gladys's house, everyone was talking about that awful news video of you being led away by a policeman. I was so embarrassed I burst into tears. Thank goodness for true friends. *They* understood my suffering and shame caused by that public exposure and assured me my reputation wasn't compromised by your actions."

"Well, Momma, I'm sorry about the video, but I can't control the news media. I'm not a criminal now, never have been, and people will *not* think you and Daddy raised one. Maybe you'd be happier if you went back to Florida now and enjoyed your retired friends there." Trying to stay calm wasn't easy. I had a mess of hurt and disappointment goin' on inside of me.

Momma sighed. "I can't go back. Not yet. Not until this awful scandal dies down. Everyone in Golden Palms has heard about it by now, I'm certain. By the way, Lottie Ferguson was at Mavis's house tonight, too. She told me Parvis had more money than King Midas. Got it through smart investing and oil. Too bad he and Poppy Rose are both gone." Momma stopped talking long enough to sip her water. That gave me a chance to slip my two cents worth into the conversation.

"Miss Nettie already told me about the Fremonts's courtship and wedding, Momma. And it's a known fact they were quite well-to-do. Sad, isn't it, the way things turned out for them? They didn't even have children." I refrained from commenting on the groom's advanced age and the possibility of little blue pills. Not a topic I wanted to discuss with Momma.

"Well, I'll bet you dollars to doughnuts that daddy of hers will have his fingers in the money pie pretty quick. I'm surprised he hasn't shown up before now."

"Momma! You always told me betting was a sin." Her statement was not at all typical of the momma I knew as a child.

"Of course, it is," she said, putting her empty glass on the table and pushing her chair back. She frowned at me. "I was using a figure of speech, Frances Louise. For goodness sakes, you should know me better than that." With a heavy sigh, she said goodnight and marched down the hall.

I recognized that tone of voice and wasn't about to pursue the conversation. "G'night, Momma," I called after her.

As soon as she went into the bathroom I hustled down the hall to the bedroom and grabbed my pajamas from the top drawer of the dresser. Keeping an eye out for Momma's return, I wiggled into them standing behind the bedroom door, trying to be quiet so as not to wake Betsy, and barefooted it back down the hallway. Could I really endure the weeks ahead with Momma underfoot? What on earth was I going to do with her while Betsy was at camp? And how would I keep her from interfering with rehearsals for the Summer Fest?

With those questions buzzing in my mind, I pulled out the sofa, fluffed my pillow, and crawled into my temporary bed. Tonight, saying my prayers would take a lot longer than usual. God and I had some serious talking to do.

Chapter Ten

Where were the kids? I stood in front of the church Thursday evening tapping my foot while I worked on controlling my nervousness. I hadn't been back inside the church since the night of the murder. Miss Nettie had told me the baptismal services scheduled for next month had been canceled until further notice. Seems some of the church members felt the baptistery needed renovating, whatever that entailed.

In light of the recent social media blitz regarding the alleged murder and my TV debut in the local reporter's video at the church, The Joyful Noise had been requested by the deacons to present a mini-preview of their musical concert. Right now those seven men were waiting in the conference room, and my singers were nowhere in sight. Nowhere!

I couldn't believe the kids were throwing away all the hard work they'd done by not showing up. Didn't they understand the importance of tonight's audition? I took one more look down the empty street before I turned and walked up the steps. The deacons had been waiting ten minutes. I owed them an explanation. With a sigh, I pulled open the door to the sanctuary.

"Yo! Teach! Wait up!"

I turned around at the shout. Six teens in camo-type clothing advanced toward me like an assault battalion on a mission. I grinned in spite of my annoyance at their late arrival. They were supposed to practice their songs after school and meet me here tonight at seven. From what they were wearing I was pretty certain they'd been shopping for outfits to wear, instead. I couldn't help smiling at the oddly assorted bunch. In my heart, they were my motley crew.

I motioned for them to hurry, relieved that they'd shown up at all. At our last rehearsal, my popularity rating took a dive when I suggested using gospel songs as the group's identifying brand of music. Their shocked expressions were enough to let me know how they really felt.

Bruno, Granville, and Wesley, wearing baggy pants and camo-printed shirts, waved and shouted hellos. Behind them, J'Nell, Joy, and Rosella hurried to catch up. Their identical Goth-black knit tank tops, ankle-length camo-print skirts, and black rubber flip-flops were only outclassed by the green, glittery polish adorning their fingernails and toenails.

J'Nell and Joy had very different fashion tastes for twins. J'Nell sported a nose ring, smudged, dark eye makeup, and black streaks in her blond, spiked hair. Joy's appearance was softer and innocent of any makeup. Her straight, darker-blond hair was shoulder-length and pulled back with a green plastic headband.

Rosella, much smaller and younger than the twins, had to hike up her skirt to keep it from dragging on the ground when she ran. A dark cap of tight, springy curls covered her perfectly-shaped head, complimenting her beautiful *café au lait* skin. A few more years and Wow! She'd be a knockout beauty.

"I see y'all have been shopping at *Twice Loved* again. Great outfits, by the way."

"Yes, ma'am. Thank you." The girls whirled around in unison, twirling their skirts. Embarrassed, the guys looked at the ground, but I didn't miss their sly grins.

I could certainly understand the hardships these teens were experiencing, financial as well as social. Their fashion choices didn't bother me a bit. They were dealing with a truckload of baggage brought about by the circumstances of their birth. No one gets to choose where they come from, but they do have the choice of where they're going in life. I had high hopes of helping them get rid of that junk while I dumped my own at the same time.

My main reason for coming home to Ruby Springs was to redeem myself. Organizing The Joyful Noise has just sort of fallen into my lap, and I couldn't be happier about that. I only hoped and prayed my recent entanglements with the law wouldn't cause problems. The police hadn't done much to further their investigation besides cordon off the mansion and stir up speculation. No wonder the deacons were concerned.

"Well, let's get a move on. Another minute and you would've had to find your own way to the deacons' meeting without me." I tempered my scolding with a grin.

"Wow, you're really scarin' us, Miz Frankie Lou." The boys screwed up their faces in fake horror, rolled their eyes, and pretended to die on the spot by falling on the ground. *Yeah, right.*

I pooh-pooh'd their dramatics and got right down to business. "Hey, I'm serious, y'all. Listen up. I'm hoping the deacons will be impressed by your singing tonight. That's the whole reason for this singing preview. They already decided to let us use the fellowship hall for rehearsals, but remember, they have the power to revoke that decision. If that happens, we'll have to keep squeezing together in my house."

The teens groaned. My house was seriously tiny. Put six rambunctious teens, an old, used guitar, and a rickety keyboard inside and the seating arrangement rivaled the tightest-packed canned sardines. Our last rehearsal had been a challenge.

Bruno spoke up. "Oh, we're ready, Miz Frankie Lou. Honest. I brought my guitar to school on my lunch break from work today so we could practice in the school parking lot." He grinned, a wonderfully engaging grin. "Snagged a fine audience, too, and didn't even get run off by the security guard, neither."

Tall and muscular at eighteen, Bruno Brown was the oldest of the kids. He had appointed himself the pseudo-leader and protector of the rag-tag musical group. He'd dropped out of high school his senior year to get his GED and go to work for a local rancher, but insisted his younger brother stay and finish his education. Life was tough for a young black man in this small Texas town. Jobs were scarce, but Bruno was determined to provide a better future for his kid brother.

Granville Brown brushed his mass of black dreads from his shoulder and shot a wide grin Frankie Lou's way. "Yeah, I stashed my keyboard in Wesley's locker 'cause it's closer to the side exit than mine. We skipped out early and snuck down the hall past old man Crowder's office slicker'n snot." The two boys did some sort of mysterious hand-jive with each other and bumped chests. The girls burst into a fit of giggles.

"I understand how you feel, Granville," I said, shaking my head at his graphic description, "but the deacons might not appreciate those colorful words tonight." *This boy's manners need a heap of work.* Still, my heart swelled at the obvious eagerness these kids possessed for singing. The chance to show off their musical talents in public would be a dream come true for them. At school, they'd been called "weird" and "trailer trash" for so long they'd finally quit fighting back and were seriously thinking about dropping out altogether, like Bruno had. I wouldn't let that happen. The kids had potential, and I was determined to push them to the height of success. I had dreams, too.

"Just remember, y'all, this is a church, so be respectful. Now let's go in and show the deacons what you can really do with your voices. We want to convince them they made the right decision by letting us rehearse at the church." I opened the door, and the motley group followed me inside.

The boys hung back to let the girls go in first. It wasn't their good manners, though, but the uncertainty of things to come. Whispering, all six dragged their feet like they were slogging through quicksand. I figured they hadn't been inside a church recently, if ever, and hoped they weren't too intimidated to perform well for the deacons.

"Get the lead out, gang. We have a song to sing for the deacons. And stop worrying. Trust me, you'll be great." *Look who's talking*, my conscience prodded.

The doubtful look in their eyes made me all the more determined to carry out my plan. Herding the group quietly through the sanctuary and past the baptistery, their whispers grew louder, and I heard the words *murder* and *cops*. How much did they know? Did they think I had something to do with it? The whispering continued.

"*This* is where it happened, y'all. Where that woman was killed." The voice sounded like J'Nell's, but I couldn't be certain. One of the boys, most likely Granville, whispered back, "Kinda creepy. Wonder what God thinks about having a murderer in the church?"

"Guess he'd know who done it and prob'ly gonna send down a lightning bolt and strike 'em dead."

"But the cops haven't found—"

All whispering stopped when I opened the door to the choir room. "No matter what you've heard about the unfortunate death here the other evening or what your opinion is, let's put gossip aside and concentrate on performing well tonight, okay?"

Six heads nodded. I hoped they understood. I left instructions to practice quietly until I came to get them.

On my way across the hall to the larger room where the deacons waited to meet The Joyful Noise for the first time, I said a prayer for extra heavenly help. I hoped God would be generous.

After making a brief introductory speech to the deacons and thanking them again for their support, Mr. Botts stood and motioned for me to take a seat. My heart ker-flopped. Were the deacons changing their mind?

"Frankie Lou, there's a matter of grave concern the deacons need to discuss with you before we hear your group."

I nodded, afraid if I spoke I'd be on my knees begging the men not to judge the singers by anything I had done. "What is it, Mr. Botts?" I clasped my hands in my lap to keep from biting my fingernails.

"Some if our church members are alarmed by the negative publicity the church has gotten regarding the death of our choir director and are having second thoughts about hosting your group inside the church."

I jumped to my feet. "But Mr. Botts," I cried, "the kids have nothing to do with what happened here."

The senior deacon waved me back to my seat. "We know that, Frankie Lou, and to be fair, because we promised, we've agreed to let the kids speak for themselves in song. If you'll bring them in now, we're ready to hear them. We just want you to know that we're under pressure to cancel."

"Thank you, gentlemen. You won't regret giving the kids a chance." With that, I hurried to the practice room to collect the singers. My hand froze on the door knob.

From inside the room, a crazy Elvis-uh-huh version of *This Little Light of Mine* pounded through the walls. Bruno's guitar riffed, and Wesley's baritone did amazing things with the melody. But that was not the version we'd rehearsed. If the deacons heard them singing rock 'n'roll, we'd be tossed out after the first verse. Seriously. This had to stop before The Joyful Noise blew their chances of entering the competition all to heck and back.

I rushed in waving my hands. "Whoa, kids! Stop right now!" The music stopped faster than if I'd pulled their power plug.

Six pairs of eyes looked at me like I'd lost my everlovin' mind.

Bruno spoke up, embarrassment flushing his face. "I can explain, Miz Frankie Lou."

"Well, I certainly hope so," I said. "Are y'all deliberately trying to get us kicked out of here? Remember, no rock and roll and absolutely NO hand-jiving or hip-hop, you hear me?" Hands on my hips, I took stock of the kids' disheartened expressions and reality *whomped* me good upside my head. I had turned into my momma.

Here I was dissing their efforts instead of supporting them. Their faces fell clear to their toes, and they looked so dejected I paused and had a major brain session honestly assessing the situation. This new version really did sound better than the way we'd originally rehearsed. It packed a punch that was sure to get the approval of the deacons' board.

Bazinga! The kids had the right idea, after all. Gospel music should be joyful, and that's exactly what their singing represented—joyful noise. They'd understood the purpose of their music, while I'd been too concerned about conforming to old-fashioned rules to realize the true value of their talents went way beyond their voices.

"Kids, I am so sorry I hollered at y'all. I guess the shock of hearing something so completely different from what I'd expected sort of blindsided me for a minute. Your arrangement is perfect for the competition. We'll definitely use it. And you can try it out on the deacons right now." I held my breath waiting for their reaction.

Heads jerked up, and smiles spread like summer sunshine across their faces. Then they all talked at once like a bunch of mockingbirds on speed.

"You had us scared for a minute there, Miz Frankie Lou," Granville said, tugging nervously on one of his dreads.

"So, you didn't really mean all that stuff about getting kicked out, after all?" one of the twins asked.

"Nah, she was just jokin'," Wesley piped in. "Weren't you, Miz Frankie Lou? You said you liked how we sang."

"Yes, I did, Wesley. It's exactly right. You don't even have to tone it down, just keep it the way you want tonight and see how the deacons react, but I'm not joking about making a good impression, kids. We'll be in the deep stuff if they don't let us use the church for rehearsal, so this performance can make or break the deal. As long as you don't even think about asking what the fox says, you'll be golden."

That powered another outburst of *Hoorahs*, and their smiles told me I was forgiven. But the sinking sensation in my belly made me wonder if I'd have regrets later, the same as I'd had after seeing Poppy Rose's lifeless body beneath the water in the baptistery.

"Somethin' wrong, Miz Frankie Lou? All of a sudden you're looking kinda' pale. Maybe you should sit down."

Bruno set his guitar aside and walked over. Though he towered over me, there was genuine concern in his soulful, dark eyes. He meant well. I didn't know much about him, only that his rocky past had made him protective of those he considered his friends. I hoped I was one of those friends now. It was important for all the group members to trust me. And today's incident made me realize I needed to trust them, too.

"I'm fine, Bruno. Just a little nervous about tonight, that's all."

"We promise not to screw it up, Miz Frankie Lou, honest." He turned to the others. "Don't we, gang?"

The teens nodded and crossed their hearts. "We promise." The excitement in their eyes and bright smiles were all the reassurance I needed. How could anyone doubt that kind of sincerity?

Minutes later, The Joyful Noise faced the deacons with those same smiles as they waited for their cue from Bruno's guitar intro. The chords his nimble fingers strummed on that old Gibson couldn't have been sweeter. I had no clue how he came to possess the instrument, but it reinforced my belief in the power of Divine intervention. If the angels are listening this evenin', I'm pretty sure they've got Bruno in their sights as a candidate to accompany their Heavenly choir someday.

The Joyful Noise swung into the traditional rendition of *This Little Light of Mine*. Classic, respectable, sure to impress. I blew out a sigh of relief. They were doing themselves proud with the straight-up, by-the-book performance, but where was their original arrangement? The one I agreed they could use? The one I knew would show their true talents?

A smattering of applause began as the men nodded their approval, but to everyone's surprise, the singers weren't finished. They never missed a beat when Bruno picked up the tempo. I shot a wide-eyed look from Bruno to Wesley and mouthed *What's going on?*

The whole group grinned and executed a perfectly synchronized transition from straight gospel right into rock and roll. Not the music I'd just heard in the practice room. No, this was their unique rendition of *Old-Time Religion* with moves as smooth as anything Usher might have personally choreographed.

I grinned until my face hurt. You saw it first right here at Faith Community Church, folks. God love 'em, those kids performed that first song pure and simple, the way I'd wanted. How could I be anything but proud of their enthusiasm for this old favorite? Then they'd respectfully jazzed it up to show the deacons that gospel music could be fun as well evangelistic. This wasn't the song I'd heard earlier in the choir room. No, this was even better. I couldn't sit still. I wanted to (*Shout*) kick my heels up and (*Shout*) throw my hands up and (*Shout*) throw my head back and—well, you know how the rest of that goes.

By the time they sang the last note, there was so much old-time religion in the air, every deacon was clapping his hands and tapping his foot. Matter of fact, when the song ended, the men gave the singers a rousing standing O! I jumped up and down, clapping so hard my hands stung.

Every single one of the kids flashed a bright smile as they bowed to their audience, but I knew they were holding their breath.

"Well, gentlemen, you've just met The Joyful Noise singers," I said, my heart filled with so much pride I thought it might burst. "They wanted you to be the first to hear their presentation before the fundraiser performance for the public next week as a thank you for giving us a place to rehearse. We promise to put it to good use on Thursday nights and be respectful in God's house."

The kids all nodded their agreement. Granville crossed his fingers behind his back.

When the applause ended, the deacons huddled together briefly before Deacon Botts stepped forward. "We are unanimous in our vote of confidence, Frankie Lou," he said. "You have a fine group, and we're happy to give them our support. However, we must ask you to postpone the fundraiser concert until after Poppy Rose's funeral. I'm sure you understand."

I assured the deacons we would abide by their wishes. Every one of the singers loudly voiced their agreement.

After the closing prayer, the deacons shook hands with the singers. Then the kids pulled me into a group hug and, swear to goodness, that was the best feeling I'd had in a long time.

"Way to go, kids. I'm so proud of you," I said and swiped away a pesky tear. "So, what happened to the song you were singing in the choir room? You sure surprised me with that second song. And when did you have time to practice those awesome moves?"

J'Nell piped up, her bright eyes sparkling. "The dancing was the easy part. We knew how much you wanted us to sing a real gospel song, so we decided to sing two and add a little extra to the last one. The one you heard was a new arrangement we just started working on. We already had tonight's presentation all planned." She laughed. "You should've seen the look on your face when we started the second song."

"Yeah, your mouth dropped open so far it 'bout hit the floor," Granville said, his grin just as infectious as his older brother's.

"Well, the performance was priceless. I'm so proud of you. Now, y'all are free to go on home, but remember to be here Thursday evening at seven. We'll work on your songs for the fundraiser. Hopefully, Miss Nettie and I will have time to decide on a costume for you by then. The funeral for Miz Fremont isn't until Tuesday."

"Why can't we just wear our cool camo stuff like tonight?" Granville pointed to what they were wearing. "We don't need nothin' else."

"But we want something new for the competition," J'Nell and Joy protested in unison.

"'Course you do," Granville said. "You're girls."

Laughing, J'Nell punched him on the arm.

Granville grabbed his arm and moaned dramatically. "Hey, that hurt! Not fair. You know I don't hit no little girls."

"And *you* know we're not little girls, dude." J'Nell had her fist ready to pop him one again.

I stepped in between the two and held up my hands. "Truce, okay? Tell you what, gals and guys, you can wear the camo gear next week at the fundraiser concert, and if enough money comes in from donations, we'll get you new outfits, too. That way you'll have two costume changes for the Summer Fest competition. Talk it over this week and come up with some ideas by next Thursday's rehearsal, okay? Now, go straight home. No dilly-dallying. That'll just get you in trouble. I'll see you back here at the church on Thursday."

I waved them out the front door, and they took off, all jazzed up by the deacons' praise like the happys had taken hold of them. Later, after I'd thanked the deacons one more time, my own feet did a joyful skip all the way home. My mood would've only been better if I'd had someone to share it. However, my mental image of Joe Camps and his sexy grin was a mighty poor substitute for the real deal.

I'd learned that Joe's prison time had a heartbreaking explanation. He'd taken the rap for his younger brother in a gas station robbery. Joe had followed the brother, who had a drug habit, and tried to stop him before the crime happened but got there too late. The brother ran, leaving Joe at the scene with the stolen money and an unfired gun when the police arrived.

Joe deserved a lot of happiness after what he'd been through.

FRIDAY BREEZED by filled with plenty at work to keep me jumping. Even Doc was exhausted when five o'clock came around. The nicest part of the day came when Doc surprised me by agreeing to keep Lucky as the clinic's mascot. We'd had no luck finding his owner, and as much as I wanted him for Betsy, I knew he'd be better off with Doc. The two had bonded immediately like long lost friends.

At ten minutes after five, I said goodbye to my employer and closed the clinic behind me, ready to head home. I dreaded another night listening to Momma beat the dead horse known as 'my irresponsible lifestyle', so I was actually glad when Detective Hardy phoned me shortly after I arrived home, even though he politely requested my immediate presence for more questioning. Fortunately, Momma had already left to take Betsy out for dinner and some last minute shopping afterwards for camp clothes. They planned to make an evening of it. *Un*fortunately, Miss Nettie was at the house when I got the call, and no amount of arguing could keep her from accompanying me downtown.

I took my sickly minivan in deference to my arthritic neighbor and parked in the lot across from the police station, knowing there'd be plenty of security and lighting. I'd probably be farther ahead if someone stole the dying van.

We exited the elevator on the second floor, and the sergeant on duty ushered us down the hall. Miss Nettie was in her glory, peeking into every room we passed that had an open door. Once she boldly opened a door marked *Do Not Enter*, setting off an ear-splitting alarm and sending the sergeant scrambling to report the misfire. I recognized trouble as soon as I saw a scowling Detective Hardy waiting for us outside his office door.

Miss Nettie scooted past the detective ahead of me and grabbed the chair nearest his desk. "Detective, I'm Frankie Lou's neighbor and here to help any way I can. Don't know why you called her in, but I can tell you she didn't kill Poppy Rose, and that's a fact. Seems to me you fellows need to speed up your investigating."

Hardy was still fuming when he reentered the room. I held my breath when he stopped beside Miss Nettie's chair and hoped he'd be gentle in his reprimand. After all, she hadn't meant any harm.

"I know who you are, Miss Bloom, and I assure you this meeting is not a public forum. I'll have to ask you to leave before you set off any more alarms and disrupt the entire building."

Miss Nettie huffed indignantly, like she hadn't done anything wrong. "Like I said, I'm here on behalf of Frankie Lou. I'll leave when she does."

Oh, that'll help me out, neighbor. "Detective Hardy, unless you're going to arrest me, I wish you'd let Miss Nettie stay. It's too far for her to walk back home, and really, I don't have anything to hide from her or anyone else." I didn't know if my pleading would help or hinder my status with the law, but I had to try. I didn't want Miss Nettie to be in any trouble because of me, bless her misdirected good intentions.

Hardy moved away to sit behind his desk, taking his own sweet time to sort through the papers there. Finally, he looked up, and once more I held my breath. "You can stay on one condition, Miss Bloom. Don't say a word until you have my permission. Understand?"

Miss Nettie nodded demurely, the picture of a properly chastised older lady. Lord save us from senior showtime. Her acting skills were on a roll.

"There must be something important for my summons, Detective." Tired of waiting for a proper explanation and more than a little antsy as to what might be ahead, I cautiously pushed for an answer.

"Very important, Miz McMasters. You see, the victim's car was found abandoned just outside of town with her empty purse inside. Can you remember anything else about the vehicle you claim tried to run you down in the church parking lot the night of the accident?"

"I've told you everything, Detective. I thought it was Poppy's car, but it couldn't be. I never saw the driver."

"Sounds like a kidnapping gone wrong—you *know* how rich Poppy was," Miss Nettie piped up, nearly sending me into shock.

"Miss Nettie, you promised," I whispered, but my frantic warning went unheeded, and she continued to badger him.

"Tell me, Detective, did your super-duper crime squad find any ransom notes when they were out there scurrying around the mansion like squirrels burying nuts? Did they?"

"Please, Miss Nettie." I grasped her arm and tried not to squeeze too hard. "No talking, remember?" I groaned. She had just pounded more nails in my coffin. I waited for Detective Hardy to sink the final one.

Sometimes the unexpected can turn out to be a good thing. Miss Nettie's plucky, outspoken style made it happen when she coaxed a half-smile from the grim-faced detective.

"Miss Nettie, with all due respect to your age, you're a fine piece of work," Detective Hardy said, holding back a full grin. "No wonder Miz McMasters brought you along this evening."

Relief washed over me like a welcome rain shower in a drought. Who would've thought my gutsy, elderly friend would end up getting us a reprieve?

Chapter Eleven

After our visit with Detective Hardy at the police station, Miss Nettie insisted on stopping for ice cream on our way home. Never one to pass up a chance for a hot fudge sundae, I found a parking space along the street, and we joined the waiting line at the walk-up window.

"You'd think they'd have two windows open, wouldn't you? Look how many people are standing here waiting to order." Miss Nettie clearly didn't like waiting for her ice cream. I agreed.

"But there's only room for one window along the wall," I said. "Guess we'll have to wait our turn or go without."

"Pshaw! I know that, child. I just like to grumble sometimes. One of the perks of gettin' old. I'm still put out by what that detective fellow said. The very idea telling me to be quiet or go home. That's exactly why I spoke up like I did. Got the old sourpuss grinning, too, didn't I? Don't know what the big secret was. He never said another word about the murder after he'd told us about finding Poppy Rose's car. Huh! He could've said that over the phone."

I nodded. I'd been thinking along that same line. I felt there was something more he'd wanted to say if she hadn't been sitting there, but I wasn't about to mention that. We moved up the line, Miss Nettie clapping when we reached the order window.

"I'll have two scoops of Cherry Chip," Miss Nettie said, pushing up close to the window like she feared losing her place in line. "In a cone."

Because a sundae would mean sitting down at one of the outside picnic tables and I was anxious to get home, I ordered a small cone of vanilla. By the time I pulled into my driveway, we both had finished our cones.

"Looks like Momma and Betsy are still shopping," I said, stopping the car midway up the drive.

Miss Nettie grabbed her pocketbook and patted my shoulder. "Ta-ta, Frankie Lou. I'll see you tomorrow after I watch my morning TV shows." She started out of the car and stopped with a jerk, nearly choked by the still-fastened seat belt.

I leaned over and released it. "Are you all right?"

She laughed, waving off her forgetfulness as she scurried down the sidewalk to her pretty little home. I waited until she was safely inside before parking the van in the garage and closing the overhead door. "What a night," I muttered as I entered the house. I hoped Momma and Betsy were having a good time. I left my sandals by the door and headed for the kitchen. The notion about robbery as a motive for Poppy's death bothered me. Something didn't add up, and until I figured it out I could use a few minutes of quiet "me" time for uninterrupted thinking.

I grabbed a bottle of water from the fridge and crashed on the couch with my feet up. My cell phone interrupted my "me" time. Charlie Daniels and his fiddle can't be ignored. I answered the darn thing.

"Frances Louise, is that you?"

"Yes, Momma, it's me. What's wrong?" *Please, not an accident with Betsy in the car.*

"Nothing's wrong. I decided to treat Betsy to a movie, since there's a seven o'clock showing of one she wants to see. We'll be home no later than nine-thirty. Don't lock us out."

"That's fine, Momma. Have fun. See you when you get home."

She hung up without saying goodbye, but that didn't surprise me. I disconnected, grabbed my purse from the bedroom, and was back on the road quick as a jackrabbit. I'd just been granted a couple of hours to revisit the church parking lot in hopes of finding some answers. The cops were taking their own sweet time with the investigation, and I was becoming more and more impatient for the crime to be solved. Even the singing group was beginning to ask questions. How could I be a role model if I'm a suspect in a murder?

I eased out of the driveway hoping Miss Nettie was watching *Wheel of Fortune* and wouldn't see me leave. I left my van just inside the church parking lot and walked to the back of the lot where Poppy's car had been parked in her favorite spot, the safety zone near the dumpster, to avoid nicks and scratches on her car.

There was still enough daylight for me to see clearly, so I checked out the area around the industrial-sized dumpster for anything the police might have missed. The paved parking lot was bare of any bits of trash, and the strip of grass behind the dumpster yielded nothing suspicious, either—not that I had any idea what I was looking for.

I was tempted to lift the cover of the container and had just reached for the handle when I saw the blood. At least, I thought that's what it was. I looked closer, sniffed, and sure enough, there was dried blood on the corner. How had the cops missed it? This must be where Poppy hit her head, not in the baptistery like the cops said.

Puzzled, I continued walking around the dumpster, my head filled with questions. If it was a simple robbery, wouldn't the robber just toss her inside the dumpster? Why take her inside the church? My suspicions grew when I thought about how I'd barely missed being run down by the person who killed Poppy Rose. Fear that it could happen again helped me make the decision to call the detective and tell him what I'd discovered. I took my phone from my purse and punched the number the detective had given me after my first Q & A with him and Chief Jackson. Fortunately, I had it on speed dial.

After sharing my findings and answering more questions, I went home. Momma and Betsy arrived thirty minutes later. I only mentioned the callback by Detective Hardy and stopping for ice cream with Miss Nettie. I figured my personal efforts to clear my name were on a need-to-know basis to Momma and Miss Nettie. For their good and mine. Especially mine.

THE DAY OF POPPY Rose's funeral arrived right on schedule, thanks to the police department's early release of the body. There'd been no official press statement from Chief Jackson and no arrests made, so speculation was running high among Ruby Springs's citizens as to the reason for the decision. Most of them were betting on their first suspect—me.

If you'd told me two weeks ago I'd be attending the funeral of Poppy Rose Fremont today, I would've laughed. If you'd told me she'd been the victim of a homicide and I was the number one person of interest, I'd have called you plumb crazy. And if you'd told me Momma would still be here organizing my life and giving me grief about my "little trouble" with the police, my weight, and everything else about my lifestyle, I would have happily sent her home to live with you. Today, my emotions teetered precariously on the edge of downright dangerous, and I dared anyone to look cross-eyed at me once I walked into the church, aka the scene of the crime.

Looking at the crowd of mourners seated around me this Tuesday morning, I noticed most of Ruby Springs's population had gathered to pay their respects. I wondered who was minding the shops. Every pew in Faith Community was packed with both church members and the just plumb curious.

In the sanctuary, the cloyingly sweet scent of lilies mingled with the heavy fragrance from dozens of roses blanketing the casket. I sat at the back of the church to view those in attendance. If I'd been seated any closer to the abundance of floral arrangements, my head would've exploded from the *eau de funeral* fragrances. When I realized part of the airborne pathogen was Momma's cologne, I moved to the end of the pew nearest the aisle and wiped my stinging eyes.

Seated at the organ, Emma Jean Botts softly filled the sanctuary with a solemn rendition of *Rock of Ages* while the choir, minus their deceased director, added their voices to the hymn from their place to the right of the pulpit. One by one, the deacons filed slowly past the pews to take their place in front of the mourners.

"They're the pall-bearers," Momma whispered, as if that needed explaining. She scooted over closer to me, bringing her nasal-burning fragrance with her.

"Yes, I know, Momma," I whispered back. "Deacon Hadley made all the arrangements. Looks like he bought up all the lilies in the county. Those garlands of poppies and twinkling lights draped over the baptistery curtains are downright hideous. The whole thing looks like a circus side show." I shuddered at the carnival-like atmosphere.

I'd attended more than one funeral at Faith Community while we lived in the parsonage. After all, Daddy had served as pastor here for many years, and Momma and I were expected to attend each and every church function. That's just the way it was. However, none of the affairs had been as over-the-top tacky as the hoopla being made over today's service for Poppy Rose. Where were Poppy's parents? And why on earth had Deacon Hadley been put in charge? Miss Nettie had told me his appointment to the Board of Deacons had come about at Parvis Fremont's influential suggestion but before that he'd been quiet as a mouse in the community.

Beside me, Momma frowned her disapproval of my commentary and squirmed around in the pew like a toddler with an overactive bladder. Ever since we sat down, she'd been checking out the late comers to speculate on who'd be staying for the luncheon after the service, better described as the central gossip exchange. I sighed. I'd forgotten just how important such things were to her. Did she miss all this local socializing in her new Florida community of over-50's couples?

Momma, who had never followed fashion trends in her life and didn't know jack about designer clothes when we lived in the parsonage, was busy eyeballing the church ladies' latest outfits. She certainly gave them a run for their money dressed in her tropical Florida finery, which, by the way, took some getting used to. I suspected more than her appearance had changed since she'd left Ruby Springs. I wondered how Daddy was adjusting.

I craned my neck and did a quick search for Miss Nettie. She should've been here by now. Earlier, I had offered her a ride with us in Momma's rental car, but she wasn't quite ready to leave. She'd assured us she would catch a ride with Lovey Muchmore, the church secretary, so I promised to save her a seat. Where was she?

The sanctuary was filling fast. The people were scrunched together in the pews with barely room to breathe. The thought that someone in the crowd could be Poppy's killer was never far from my mind. So far, everyone who'd entered the church was a member of Faith Community or a business owner. Not a stranger in the bunch.

Divinity Pettibone, who sold organic beauty products at home demonstration parties, swished down the aisle in a skin-tight black dress, its plunging neckline better suited for a red carpet affair than a somber funeral. She pushed her way into the pew directly in front of us, but not before she shot a nervous glance my way. Miss Nettie was right behind her, grinning like a cat with a bathtub full of sweet cream. I didn't see Lovey with her, though.

My little neighbor nudged me. "Scoot over," she whispered a little too loudly.

"Where's Lovey? Didn't you ride with her?"

"She left after she dropped me off. Had a dental appointment she couldn't change, she said." Miss Nettie squeezed her way into the pew. I tapped Momma on the shoulder, and we both slid over to make room.

My nose twitched as a fleeting trace of a familiar scent alerted my nasal warning system. Miss Nettie? No, she always used that traditional almond-scented lotion. *Oops!* My suppressed sneeze came out in an unladylike snort. Who, then? I leaned forward and sniffed once more. This time I sneezed loud enough to make heads turn. Bingo! Divinity Pettibone wore the same fragrance as the blond floozie who brought the injured mutt into the clinic for treatment and left without paying her bill. Could there be a connection?

Before I could lean over the pew to ask Divinity the name of her unusual fragrance, Reverend Whitlaw approached the pulpit to begin the final service for Poppy Rose Fremont.

Momma silenced me with an elbow in my ribs and a *Shush*! Miss Nettie whispered something in my ear about not seeing Poppy Rose's folks at the service, but before I could answer her the Reverend reminded us why we were there and started praying. In spite of our differences in the past, saying goodbye to Poppy Rose this way left me sad and full of regrets.

LATER, AS I LEFT the committal service at the cemetery with Miss Nettie trotting along behind me hanging on to Momma's arm, I noticed a man and woman standing apart from the crowd. Something about their nervous demeanor struck me as odd, as if they were trying to avoid being seen. Call it intuition or just curiosity, but I wanted to take a closer look at the couple's faces.

Without giving away my intention, I informed Momma and Miss Nettie that I'd seen a friend I wanted to speak to and would meet them at the car shortly. I left them to weave my way through the departing mourners, trying not to look obvious as I hurried toward the couple.

Well, Lord love a duck! Even with an expensive-looking Stetson shading his face, I recognized the burly figure of Ruby Springs's ex-mayor, Poke deHaven. Sure enough, Poppy Rose's daddy had come to see his daughter buried. The woman clinging to his arm had momentarily turned away from me so I couldn't get a clear view of her face. Ever curious, I moved toward them. I'd almost reached them when my nose twitched and . . . *ACHOOooo!*

Poke's lady friend turned at the sound. Stunned, I stared into the equally surprised, heavily made-up face of the blond who'd left her dog and an unpaid bill at Doc's clinic.

Poke grabbed her hand, and the two took off walking so fast over and around the graves of the silent residents of the Rock of Ages Cemetery, you'd have thought their shiny shoes had wings. I lit out after the fleeing pair like a chicken after a June bug.

"Hey, Mr. deHaven! Wait!" I zig-zagged through the grave sites, dodging flabbergasted mourners and astonished deacons as I ran. I had no idea what I'd say or do if I caught up with the couple; I only knew I had to find out why they were so eager not to be seen.

My foot caught the corner of a headstone when I turned too quick, and I went down hard on my hands and knees. By the time I righted myself, my knees skinned and hurting, I'd lost sight of Poke and his lady. Huffing and puffing, I stopped when I reached the paved street that wound in and out of the cemetery plots and looked around. Poke and his lady friend were nowhere to be seen. How could they have disappeared so fast? The only places they could've hidden were behind the vaults scattered among the smaller grave sites, and none of those were accessible to the public. There'd been no passing cars, as the mourners were just now reaching their vehicles and preparing to drive out of the cemetery.

I spun around at the sound of running footsteps behind me. I don't know who I expected to see, but I should've been suspicious when I sneezed again.

Sure enough, Divinity Pettibone caught up to me fast as her skin-tight dress would allow, gasping for words between breaths. "Which way did they go?"

"Hold on a minute, Divinity," I said. "I need to sit and catch my breath before I keel over." My own heart still thudded from the exertion of the chase. A sudden, sharp pain stabbed my side. Doubled over like an arthritic ninety-year-old, I made it over to an iron bench near the edge of the section of graves and plopped down. "That was Poke deHaven, wasn't it?" I pushed out my words between gasps.

"Yes, that was Poke, the jerk. Wretched man had the nerve to show up with HER! Did you see which way they went?"

Raccoon-eyed and disheveled, Divinity pulled a lace hanky out of her purse and dabbed at the fine sheen of perspiration playing havoc with her mascara.

I shook my head. "No, I lost sight of them when I fell. I don't know where they went. Who's the woman with him, Divinity? Do you know her?"

"Well, of course I know her," she snapped, patting at her perspiring upper lip with the mascara-stained hanky. "She's my younger sister, Delilah. She's supposed to be in Michigan. I've got to—" She dropped the hanky and pointed toward the cemetery entrance farther down the street, screeching "There they are!" Arms waving and still shouting, she took off after them like a goosed roadrunner.

Momma and Miss Nettie had been waiting by my van parked a short distance away, so I wasn't surprised when they came running over to see what was causing all the commotion. Divinity flew past them, leaving them shaking their heads.

"Lord love a duck, has the woman gone crazy?" Miss Nettie threw up her hands.

"Looks like it," I said.

Naturally, Momma tsk-tsked her disapproval. "Disgraceful. Screaming and running down the street in that skinny dress with her bosom bouncing all around. Shameful exhibitionist."

"She'll knock herself out with those things if she's not careful," Miss Nettie commented.

Momma didn't know what she meant, but I caught on right away. My neighbor read too many hard-boiled mysteries.

"Uh-huh," I said and nodded. The discovery that Divinity Pettibone had a sister had come as a surprise to me, but I wasn't about to open that can of worms. If the two women started digging in it, no telling what they'd pull out. I was still trying to figure out why Poppy Rose's daddy had tried to hide his presence at his own daughter's burial. And if the woman with him truly was Divinity's sister, then I'd go after her later for that unpaid bill. But first there was the mystery surrounding Poppy to solve.

With Momma and Miss Nettie in the back seat of the van, I drove away from the cemetery to pick up Betsy from her girlfriend's house. Momma was quiet for an entire block, still sulking because she'd lost the argument when I refused to make Betsy attend the funeral. I'd won that minor battle, but the war was ongoing.

Speaking of ongoing, Momma's sulk gave way to more questions I couldn't answer. By the time we dropped Miss Nettie at her house and I parked the van in my driveway, my ears were still ringing from the two women's non-stop speculation about Poke deHaven and his lady friend. Even Miss Nettie never expected him to shack up with Divinity's younger sister.

"I say he's got an insurance policy on Poppy Rose," Miss Nettie declared later, settling herself at my kitchen table while I got out glasses for iced tea. "Why else would he sneak back with that hussy?" She'd exchanged her funeral clothes for a colorful Hawaiian-print muumuu and popped back over to my house to continue the gossip session with Momma.

Momma came out of the bathroom where she'd gone to freshen up. She'd fretted about being outside in the heat all the way home from the cemetery like she was a delicate, hot house plant.

"There ought'n to be any reason for secrecy," she said, tugging the elastic waist of her polyester slacks in place. "After all, Poke is her father. He probably came for the reading of her will. You know she and Parvis never had children."

I nodded, and Momma *tsk-tsked* like she always did when something or someone didn't meet with her approval.

"But, if that's so, then why didn't he and his lady friend attend the church service? And why did he run away when I called to him at the cemetery?" I asked.

I took a pitcher of tea from the refrigerator and filled our glasses while Momma set out a plate of raw veggies and a container of hummus.

Betsy grabbed a juice box from the fridge and a cookie from a stash Momma hadn't discovered and dashed off to her room to change into shorts and a tank top. *Smart girl.* With the temperature hovering at ninety, I was tempted to do the same.

Miss Nettie pulled a large, plastic butter tub from the fridge and set it on the table. With a grin, she opened it and took out a cookie. So much for keeping our hiding spot a secret.

"I wonder if the police found anything suspicious when they searched Poppy's house," she said and took a bite of cookie.

Momma frowned when she saw the cookies. I ignored her and dipped a celery stick in the hummus. The cookies would have to wait until after she went to bed tonight.

"I imagine they scoured the house and grounds thoroughly," I said. "Seems odd to have the funeral service before the investigation is over, unless the police have enough evidence to arrest someone and haven't revealed it to the media." *As long as it wasn't me!*

I sampled the celery and hummus. Not bad, but it will never replace chocolate chip cookies in my kitchen.

"Where was Parvis living when he met Poppy Rose?" I asked Miss Nettie, figuring she'd know. "And had he been married before? I never heard much about him before the wedding."

Momma set her glass of tea on the table and leaned forward, ready for more gossip. "Yes, Nettie, what was his background? The deHavens wanted everyone to think he'd fallen madly in love with Poppy on that singles' cruise, but I never believed that for a minute. Why, he was much older than Poppy. And with all his money, he could've had any woman more suited to his social standing. If you ask me, Poppy Rose seduced him. Married him for his money. Shameful."

I about choked on my celery when Momma said *seduced*. And she hadn't even blinked. Sweet mercy, what other surprises were heading my way?

Miss Nettie pounded on my back until I stopped coughing out of self-defense. "Your momma's right, Frankie Lou," she said. "Poke had a roving eye and a gambling problem. Pearlene was tired of shopping at second-hand shops while he spent their savings on wine, women and song." She rolled her baby-blues. "On second thought, I'm not sure about the 'song' part, but after Poke lost that last election, he up and declared bankruptcy. Pearlene gave him his walkin' papers so fast it was over and done before most folks knew about it. Then she set out to find herself a rich replacement, only Poppy Rose beat her to it when she latched on to Parvis. That really ticked off her momma."

"Pearlene did all right after that, though," Momma pointed out. "I heard she signed up with an online dating agency and got matched with a wealthy rancher down near Houston." She rolled her eyes.

"No, that one didn't work out," Miss Nettie said. "She finally found an oil man out in West Texas and left town right after Poppy's big wedding. Nobody's seen hide or hair of her since."

"*Humph.*" Momma shrugged. "Does anyone know if she married the oil man?"

Miss Nettie's face went blank. There was a good reason for her undisputed title as the town's Information Station. She knew more about the secrets of Ruby Springs than anyone else in town, and normally loved to share that knowledge with anyone who'd listen, but all of a sudden she'd shut down the gossip party line.

Momma's eyes widened. "You know something, don't you, Nettie?" She shook a finger right in Miss Nettie's face. "Tell me right now! Is it about Frances Louise?"

"Momma! Don't be rude. My goodness, I've never heard you talk like that."

Momma turned on me then, her voice rising. "Well, how in the world do you expect me to get you out of trouble if I don't know what's been going on in town since I left?"

I pushed my chair away from the table and stood. "Gossiping won't help me or anyone else, Momma. If anything, interfering will cause more harm."

Miss Nettie shook her head. "Never mind, Frankie Lou. Your momma's got a right to ask." She leaned toward Momma. "Yes, Louisa, the oil man Pearlene married was Rupert Gooding." She waited expectantly for Momma's reaction.

"I don't believe it!" Momma exploded like a firecracker, sputtering and spewing. I looked around for my phone. I wanted it handy in case I needed to call for help.

"Who is Rupert Gooding?" I asked. Lord love a duck, this was turning into a soap opera.

Momma grabbed a paper napkin and started fanning her face, which had turned ashen. "Frances Louise, please bring me a glass of water." Either Miss Nettie's news had truly shocked her or she was fixing to be sick. Real sick.

I poured a glass of lemon-cucumber water from the pitcher in the fridge and took it to her. What next, for cryin' out loud?

If Betsy hadn't stuck her head in the room right then to ask if she could have a snack and watch television, I would've gotten the answer.

But Betsy had voluntarily stayed in her room while we women talked, so to make up for ruining part of her TV time, I made microwave popcorn for her while Miss Nettie helped Momma to the bedroom, exchanging hushed conversation on the way. No matter how I strained to hear what they said, I only managed to catch a few words that made no sense.

I handed Betsy a bowl of popcorn and a glass of milk, adding the promise of double movies tomorrow night. She thanked me with a hug and sat cross-legged on the living room floor in front of the TV, a happy girl.

Miss Nettie returned to the kitchen just as I was putting the last of the leftovers in the fridge.

"Is Momma feeling better?"

"She's fine. Just worried about you, more'n she'll admit."

My head felt like a rocket ready to blast off.

Rehearsals were coming up Thursday evening with the Joyfuls, and I needed to make some decisions about the songs they'd be singing. There was also the matter of costumes for the Summer Fest contest. Betsy would be leaving for church camp next week, and I still hadn't finished marking all her clothes with name tape. The weight of what I was facing overwhelmed me. And there hadn't even been breathing room between the mystery of Poppy Rose's death still waiting to be solved and the one about Rupert Gooding that Momma and Miss Nettie had dropped in my lap just now. I needed to escape the madness.

"Miss Nettie, I'm going to take a hot shower and spend the rest of this evening chilling out with a good book. I can't deal with any more surprises tonight. Just put your dirty dishes in the sink when you leave." I massaged the base of my neck to discourage the headache hovering there. "I'll tell Betsy to lock up after you leave."

I headed for the bathroom. *Lord, give me the patience I need to cope with Momma. And, if you could, please make her go back to Florida soon. Amen and thank you.*

Chapter Twelve

Tap-tap. Tap-tap-tap. Tap-tap. Startled out of my dead-to-the-world sleep and disoriented enough to be scared, I struggled out of a disturbing dream and sat up. Something, or someone, was at the front door. The tapping grew persistently louder. I swung my legs around to get out of bed and landed rump down on the floor with a hard *whump*. Too late, I remembered where I was. Oh, yeah. Me—lumpy sofa. Momma—my comfy bed.

TAP-TAP-TAP! I heard it again, louder this time. I scrambled up off the floor, banging my toe against the leg of the sofa hard enough to bring tears to my sleepy eyes.

Rubbing my backside, I hopped on one foot to the front door and peered out into the darkness through the side window. A figure huddled in the shadows.

Too scared to turn on the porch light, I sucked in air and was ready to run for my phone when a face pushed against the window pane. A dumpling-soft, neighborly face. My heartbeat powered down to normal, leaving my stomach to deal with untying the knot of tension there.

"Hurry up, Frankie Lou," the familiar voice demanded in a squeaky whisper. "Let me in!"

My whole body shook as I blew out a sigh of relief. "Miss Nettie?"

"Well, of course it's me, child. Who else would it be? Now, open the door. It's hot as Hades out here."

A nostril-burning whiff of mothballs blew past me as my plucky neighbor rushed inside looking like a geriatric cat burglar after chomping too much catnip.

I stared at her black, long-sleeved turtleneck top, baggy pants, and clunky boots. Wisps of silver hair poked out from under a dusty black fedora that had odd bits and pieces of shrubbery clinging to it. A strange choice of clothing in this steamy spring night. Even stranger was the wrinkled shopping bag in her black gloved hands. I strongly suspected she'd been somewhere other than the local market—it had closed two hours ago at ten o'clock.

"Well, come on in, Miss Nettie," I whispered, quickly stepping aside to let her pass. "You must be sweltering in that getup."

"Mercy sakes, young lady, what took you so long to open the door? A police cruiser drove by as I was coming up the walk. They almost spotted me, but I hid in the bushes until it passed."

Well, that accounted for the leaves stuck on her hat, but it didn't account for her late-night visit.

"What brings you out at this time of night, Miss Nettie? Is everything all right?"

She brushed a wad of crushed leaves from her sleeve and stared at me like I was talking in tongues. "Of course, I'm all right. Don't tell me you forgot. I told you after the funeral I'd be here at the stroke of midnight. Figured you'd be up and waiting by now."

"The stroke of midnight? Miss Nettie, what on earth are you talking about? Who am I waiting for—Cinderella?" I whispered loud enough for her to hear me but soft enough so as not to wake Momma or Betsy. I mean, how would I ever explain my neighbor's wacky nocturnal visit? I was beginning to lean toward Momma's belief that Miss Nettie's memory bank account was more than slightly overdrawn.

"Waiting for me, of course." She propped a fist on her hip. "You want to find Poppy's killer, don't you? Well, I found something today that'll help you start the investigation right now. I said I'd bring it over at midnight. Don't want your momma sticking her nose into our investigation."

There were still a few sleepy cobwebs I needed to shake from my barely-awake brain, but I was alert enough to remember how much my neighbor loved reading mystery novels. That's why her rambling conversation tonight worried me. Maybe the heat had scrambled her brain or, God forbid, stolen it permanently.

Outside, the temperature hovered in the humid mid-eighties, making the air soggy as a wet sponge. I closed the door to keep out the night's spring heat and took Miss Nettie by the arm, leading her across the room. With one quick motion, I smoothed out the tangled bedding I'd left on the sofa.

"Sit down, Miss Nettie. Let me get you a drink of water." Little beads of perspiration were caught in the deep wrinkles of her forehead. Such an escapade in this heat couldn't be good for a woman of her age. The bright flush on her cheeks troubled me.

"I'm not thirsty." She pooh-poohed my suggestion to sit with a wave of a gloved hand. "And I'll have you know my outfit is exactly what a PI wears for undercover activities. I didn't want to be seen coming over here. I'm certain the cops have our houses under surveillance. If you paid attention, you'd know things like that."

She grinned like a cat with one paw in the fishbowl and handed me the bag. "Here, this should help get you inside, but we have to move fast so I can return it tonight before they come back."

"Miss Nettie, what do you mean? Get in *where* before *who* comes back?" I flopped down on the sofa. Keeping up with this conversation was impossible.

"Why, get in the Fremont place before those clueless cops come back, what else? I already explained all that." She cocked her head at me like I was the one confused. "Are you sure you're all right, child? You look a little dazed."

Oh, I was dazed, all right. Clueless, too, and more than a little anxious. I closed my eyes and massaged my temples. *Lord, please help me out here so Miss Nettie and I don't wind up behind bars.*

"You know, Miss Nettie, we really don't have time to play detective. We still have to decide on the costumes for the Summer Fest. That's a priority. Besides, I'm already on Chief Jackson's to-be-watched list, so I'm staying out of his way. You should, too." I covered a yawn with my hand.

With only a few days left to get The Joyful Noise singers ready for their free-will fundraising concert that could now be held on the church lawn, I still needed to choose their songs. If we were lucky, there'd be enough donations from the concert to cover the cost of costumes for the Summer Fest. If the impromptu show didn't bring in the funds we needed to pay for the materials, we'd have think of somewhere else to get the money. My shoulders sagged under the weight of the responsibility facing me.

"*Humph!* All I can say is, you're certainly no fun," she muttered under her breath and finally sat down next to me. "I'll bet Lulu wouldn't say that to Stephanie Plum."

Okaaay, that explains the midnight visit and cat burglar get-up. Miss Nettie'd been to the Ruby Springs Library again for her weekly supply of mystery novels. No wonder she was dead set on playing private investigator. I had to come up with a way to distract her pretty quick or my plans to do a little sleuthing on my own would never happen.

I opened the package on my lap and peered inside. The crumpled wad of yesterday's newspapers puzzled me.

"Miss Nettie, why are you giving me newspapers?"

"Keep looking," she said. "It's down in the bottom. I didn't want it to fall out and get lost."

"It? What is it?" I dug around in the papers until I felt something hard and pulled it out. "Huh? Miss Nettie, why are you giving me a house key?"

The shiny object hung from a shiny, gold key ring. At closer inspection, I realized the ring was fashioned in the shape of a fancy F. Really? Could it be—?

"Where did you get this, Miss Nettie?" I held my breath. "Does it belong to the Fremonts?" If this key really came from Poppy Rose's house, we were definitely in the deep stuff now.

The twinkle in my neighbor's eyes was a dead giveaway. Her whispered words confirmed my fear. "Get dressed, Frankie Lou. If we hurry, we can get inside and look around. Maybe Chief Jackson's boys missed something important. The Ruby Springs Police Department doesn't have much practice investigating murders, you know." She cocked her head. "You do want to find Poppy's killer, don't you?"

"Of course I do, but Miss Nettie, where did you get the key? Please tell me you didn't steal it."

Miss Nettie hemmed and hawed a minute or two before she got around to answering my question, and that tended to make me edgy. An image of me in the latest prison garb flitted through my mind. Was it a one-piece or two-piece outfit? Orange wasn't my best color.

When she finally got around to answering, I didn't feel any better.

"No, didn't steal it exactly," she said. "It showed up in the last batch of messages Lovey gave me for the church newsletter. She collects all the news and announcements from the members and gives them to me in a big envelope every Sunday morning after the service so I can type up the next week's newsletter.

"Last Sunday she forgot to bring the envelope with her, and I didn't get it from her until yesterday." She paused long enough to take a breath. "Anyway, the key fell out of one of those little-bitty coin envelopes like you get at the bank sometimes. Nothing else with it, though. Just a note from Lovey to put a 'Lost and Found' notice in the next newsletter and hold onto it or give it back to her. Someone must've found the key inside the church and dropped it in the box for the secretary to put in the Lost and Found. I'm pretty sure it belongs to the Fremont place. Just look at the key ring's fancy letter. I figured you'd want to take a quick look around Poppy's house before I take the key back to Lovey. Wrapping it in the newspapers seemed safer than taking a chance on losing it in my purse."

Excitement bloomed bright red on Miss Nettie's pudgy cheeks, accompanied by a twinkle of mischief in her soft, blue eyes. I was looking at trouble. She lit up like the neon sign in the window of the gift shop on Center Street, Bella's Books and Candles.

"Oh no!" My protest came out a little louder than I intended. I lowered my voice to a whisper and continued. "We are not going inside that house, Miss Nettie. Not tonight. Not any night." I got up and paced the floor to ward off the panic attack hovering just a heartbeat away. "That would be breaking the law. Besides, the police probably still have it under surveillance. You do intend to take the key back to Lovey in the morning, don't you? You can ask her if she knows who might've left it in her collection box."

I hated to squelch her adventure, but I was in enough trouble with the police already.

She rolled those blue eyes at me. "Why, Frankie Lou, I can't do that tomorrow. I'm leaving in the morning on a bus tour with the Library Ladies to do some shopping at that new outlet mall near Fort Worth. Leaving early and won't be home until way late in the evenin'. Anyway, you have the key now, so you can do the returning." She ducked her head, guilty-like, and brushed her hands off as if she was done with the whole mess. And it *was* a mess, sure as Texas has bluebonnets.

In a moment of frustration, I mumbled something less-than-ladylike and followed her to the front door. I wasn't finished talking by a long shot.

"Miss Nettie, where are you going now?" Heaven help us if she took off looking like a resurrected cat burglar from another century and started investigating alone.

"Why, I'm going back to my house, where else? Since you won't go along with my plans for tonight, you'll have to take the key to Lovey yourself. I told you I won't have time before I leave on the tour."

With that sassy retort she marched out the front door and down the walk, a round little shadow in black, bobbing along in a mothball-scented huff.

The absurdity of it bubbled up inside me, and I chuckled softly. If ever someone looked suspicious enough to catch the eye of a Ruby Springs policeman, Miss Nettie certainly did. My spunky landlady was a force to be reckoned with when she made up her mind. Unfortunately, she forgot what was on her mind some of the time.

From my doorway, I watched until she made the short distance to her home safely and went inside.

Now that I'd been wakened out of a sound sleep, my mind refused to settle down. After getting a drink of water and making a quick trip to the bathroom, I checked in on Momma and Betsy before I went back to the living room.

I plopped down on the sofa (aka my bed) and studied the mysterious key dangling from the shiny, gold ring. How many people did I know in Ruby Springs whose last name began with F? Not any who could afford solid gold key rings. No getting around it, the job of returning the thing to Lovey tomorrow was up to me, along with an explanation as to why it was in my possession. Yeah, that ought to shake up the Faith Community gossip hotline.

Darn Miss Nettie and her ideas! Her words blinked in my head like a sign on a roadside motel. I stared at the ceiling. Flopped over on my stomach. I even tried shoving my head under the pillow, but I couldn't buy sleep if I had a million dollars. My curiosity kept prodding me to consider Miss Nettie's far-fetched suggestion. Was it really possible for the police to have overlooked a clue or two in Poppy Rose's house? Let's be honest. The Ruby Springs police force wasn't exactly on the same level as the Texas Rangers. More like Mayberry with Andy and his sidekick, Barney, simply keeping the streets safe. Miss Nettie was Ruby Springs's version of Aunt Bee.

I sat up and tossed the key on the lamp table. What did it matter? I didn't even know if the darn thing belonged to the Fremont place, did I? Just because Miss Nettie planted that *what if* earworm in my head didn't mean she was right. *I will not go inside that house! I will not!* I repeated that phrase as I reached for my clothes.

Before my common sense could catch up, I dressed quickly, grabbed my pocket flashlight from its home in the drawer next to the kitchen sink, and slipped out of the house at exactly fifteen minutes after one o'clock in the freaking morning.

What? You thought I'd just return the key without checking first to see if it fit Poppy Rose's front door? Not this gal. The only way to clear my name was to find Poppy's killer. Simple as that. I wouldn't be much help to anyone behind bars. My reasoning made perfect sense. My daughter and The Joyful Noise singers were my responsibilities, and they needed me free and clear of accusations.

Not daring to turn the light on in the garage, I used the service door to take my bike outside, taking extra precaution not to make any noise as

I left the garage. The last thing I needed was for Momma to hear me. Then I walked it down the sidewalk past Miss Nettie's house. And if Miss Nettie noticed she'd insist on tagging along, sure as dogs had fleas. Thankfully, my neighbor had no barking dogs, only her big, gray tomcat, Moses.

By the time I'd biked from my house to the Fremont estate across town I was puffing like I'd done ten miles instead of the actual three. My legs ached, and I'd worked up an icky sweat. Too bad taking Minnie-the-Van had been out of the question. The racket was enough to wake up the whole neighborhood and throw Momma into a conniption fit. Nope, the van stayed put. Besides, my budget didn't include gas money.

The damp air clung to me. Not a hint of breeze anywhere to bring relief from the spring warmth. Darker than normal, the night sky hung over the cozy community like a heavy shroud. Only the old-fashioned street lamps kept the night from being blacker than a sinner's heart. Clouds had scudded in earlier, obscuring the stars and hinting at a much-needed rain. The eerie setting would make a perfect playground for a ghost or two from the Fremonts' past, if there were any hanging around.

Cursing the extra pounds responsible for my laboring lungs, I sucked in my stomach as I walked up to the gated entry to the grounds. The next few minutes were spent trying to fit the key Miss Nettie gave me into the old-fashioned iron lock. Dumb, dumb, dumber. When had it become necessary for homes to need such tight security in the residential area of Ruby Springs? No amount of forcing or twisting could make the darn key fit the lock. Like a whack upside my head, a lightbulb moment blindsided me. Not the right key!

I dropped the useless thing in my pocket and took a moment to survey the fencing on top of the brick wall enclosing the property. I needed a new plan.

I checked my watch. Momma and Betsy would still be sound asleep. I had plenty of time to look inside the house. One option—leave my bike outside the fence and try to scale the top like a mountain climber, likely snagging my pants on the wire part of the fence, or hunt for another, easier way to get inside. Brains or brawn? I had to decide and get my butt in gear.

Brains won over brawn. At least, in my head it did. Since I'd never excelled in athletics, I voted against any wall climbing. Instead, I pushed my bike slowly along the sidewalk, carefully scrutinizing the wall for any possible place where I could squeeze through the fence. If God meant for me to get inside Poppy's house, I'd find a sign.

AFTER WALKING three sides of the block that made up the Fremont estate, I hadn't found any kind of hint from above—no chinks in the brick wall or secret entrances. No magic rabbit holes to fall into. The message was clear. *Time to stop snooping and head home, Frankie Lou, before you get caught.*

I paused under the pale glow of the corner street light for one last wistful glance toward the entrance when the rattle of the heavy front gate had me backing away from the light.

From the shadows of the shrubbery along the fence, I watched the gate swing open. I held my breath, expecting to see Detective Hardy and the crime squad emerge. I couldn't have been more wrong.

Even with their heads lowered, I recognized Poke and his lady friend, Delilah. They rushed out of the gate like two cats with their tails on fire. When they stopped by a long, shiny automobile parked at the next block, I clapped my hand over my mouth to stifle a surprised yelp. The car looked like the one that had nearly run me down the night I found Poppy Rose in the baptistery. But it couldn't be. Or could it?

The gate remained open for another heartbeat before it slowly began to close. I narrowly missed being rear-ended when the heavy gate clanged shut after me. Crouched behind the nearest shrub, I wondered if my destiny was to hide in bushes from now on. The car revved its engine, and I ducked down, holding my breath until I heard it drive away from the estate.

Miss Nettie hadn't exaggerated when she described Poppy's pride and joy as a mansion. The impressive size of the structure at the top of the drive looked like a bad imitation of Scarlett's plantation, Tara, but that was just my opinion. I'm sure most people consider it a showpiece.

The whole estate must've cost the Fremonts a bundle. The grandiose Southern-style home looked as out of place here in the dry, dusty plains of West Texas as a Baptist tent revival in the Vatican. No plantations here, only sprawling cattle ranches, an occasional abandoned jackhammer from better days, and dust. Lots and lots of dust. I shrugged. Everyone to their own taste, I suppose.

If I closed my eyes, it was easy to imagine Poppy Rose out on the verandah, grandstanding for all she was worth to her minions—a crowd of curious town folks. Poppy Rose as a Southern belle made me think of

Carol Burnett playing Scarlett O'Hara.

"Ah declare," Poppy'd say with a sweep of her hands, "how kind of y'all to come to the public viewing of this mahv'lous mansion my beloved Parvis had built just for me." She always did think she was better than everyone else. Still, no matter how snobbish she'd been, she didn't deserve to die in such a horrible way.

Behind me, a rustle in the hedges along the fence pulled my imagination back to the here and now. Fists curled tight and ready to defend myself or run, I spun around and stumbled right smack over Moses! *Crimeninny Jenny!* My poor rear slammed down on the ground rattling my spinal cord like old bones. I shot the guilty party a nasty look that should've had him running for cover. Instead, his yellow-green eyes stared back at me.

"Of all the crazy . . . ! Moses, what the heck are you doing out this late?"

Mrrowww! Miss Nettie's overweight, cat sidled over for a head scratch. I didn't need any further explanation from the four-legged Casanova. Out to enjoy his regular nighttime activity, Moses was well-known in Ruby Springs by his progeny scattered throughout the neighborhoods, but his unusually late hour of carousing tonight puzzled me. Miss Nettie's house was always locked up tight enough to raise a blister by ten o'clock every night. Giving Mr. Hot-To-Trot Moses permission for an all-nighter didn't ring true.

I stood up, dusted off the seat of my capris and picked up the mini-flashlight I'd forgotten until it fell out of my pocket when I tripped.

The big cat purred again and rubbed against my ankle. His apology for scaring me spitless, I suppose. I scratched his head one more time to let him know he was forgiven. He arched his back proudly, purred his thanks, and took off up the driveway, with his tail twitching like the Big Kahuna of Kat-Man-Do. Halfway to the house he turned back and meowed a stern *Follow me, I've been here before* command. I didn't doubt that for a minute.

Chapter Thirteen

I followed the cat up the drive to the verandah. Yes, I know. I need advice from this old tomcat like he needs a trousseau, but I had the weirdest feeling Moses knew what he was doing. I had no idea if the key I held would get me inside the house, but now that I'd managed to come this far, I wasn't giving up. I needed to speed up my investigating, though. If Momma woke up before I got back home, she would be madder than a rained-on rooster.

Moses's soft paws barely made a sound as he padded across the wooden-planked front porch. He stopped in front of the main entrance. I stared at the old-fashioned lock on the door. I took the puzzling key from my pocket. This was it! Hands shaking, I pushed the key into the lock, but instead of turning smoothly, the darn thing stuck tighter than sticker-burrs on bare feet.

No amount of finagling opened the lock. Well, fudge! I shoved the key back in my pocket. I tried looking through the tall window next to the door, but heavy drapes inside blocked my view.

I figured the key's failure was the sign I'd been expecting. Not the sign I wanted, but I couldn't continue to spend any more time trying to get inside the house. I turned to leave and nearly fell over Moses, whose fuzzy bottom was parked by my feet. He let out a wail and wrapped his fluffy tail around my ankle, his persistent caterwauling growing louder.

"What? You don't think I should leave?" Asking a cat to answer my question definitely qualified me as dumber than a box of rocks. I reached down and untangled his tail from my leg.

"Give it up, big boy. There's no way I can get inside." I checked my watch. "I've been gone an hour and a half. I won't have much time even if I do find a way to get in. Momma will be waking up in a couple of hours, and I'd better be there when she does." *Great, now I'm conversing with the darned critter.*

Moses swatted at my leg and pushed. Another very insistent *Mrowww* meant no arguing. So I didn't. Maybe this tomcat version of Lassie was onto something. When he padded away from me, I took a chance and followed him.

A weak night breeze had kicked up just enough to spread the humidity around but failed to get rid of it completely. My walk around the perimeter of the estate in the muggy air had dampened my hair as well as my clothes. Now I was wet and sticky all over. Moses didn't seem to mind the weather, though. He hurried around the corner of the wide, wraparound porch, looking back only once to see if I was following. When he reached the rear entry, he stopped in front of a medium-sized pet door. Pushing with his head, he shoved the heavy, vinyl flap aside and disappeared inside the house. Well, glory be! The fella did, indeed, know his way around the Fremont estate.

Now all I had to do was figure out how the heck to get *my* round body through that little square door. Uh-huh, sure. On my hands and knees, I shoved my head through the flap and took a look. Sure enough, Moses was right there staring at me from the other side. Mose to nose, so to speak. His purr sounded rather smug to me, if that was tomcat-ly possible.

"So what's your next big idea, Mr. Smarty Cat?" I whispered. "I'll never fit through here."

Moses turned away from the opening and meowed into the empty house. Soft, little mewling noises came from behind him. So this is where Moses had been staying on his nightly outings.

I angled my head in the opening just enough to see four tiny balls of fur bouncing playfully toward their daddy. Momma Cat herded them with gentle nudges to keep them in line as the happy family greeted Papa Cat.

Watching the kittens tumble and pounce on each other, I almost forgot the real reason I was crouched down in the dark on Poppy Rose's back porch with my head in a kitty door.

"Well, Moses," I whispered through the opening, "you have a lovely family, but there's not a snowball's chance in the hot place that I can wiggle through your little private entrance. You wouldn't happen to have an unlocked, people-sized door handy, would you?"

Moses tilted his head and looked at me like I'd lost every bit of my good sense. At this point, I was ready to agree with him. He rolled his eyes upwards. *Mrroww.* I followed his gaze to the old-fashioned lock halfway above the doggie door. Head slap! Of course, dummy! The humans' door. Now my heartbeat kicked into double time. Once again, I took the key from my pocket. *Please let it fit this time. Please, please, please.*

The *snick* of a turn, a bit of a jiggle, a twist of the door knob with my free hand, and Hotdiggety! The instant the door opened, four mini-furballs attacked my legs with excited meows and tiny sharp claws. I reached down and gave Moses a grateful head scratch before scooping up a tiny yellow-and-white bundle of fluff to cradle in my arms.

"Thanks, Moses, you sneaky Casanova. Did you actually think I could fit through that critter door, or did you only want to show off your family? Either way, I'm grateful for whatever brought us together tonight."

Moses rubbed against my ankles one more time. I set the kitten down beside him. Papa Cat meowed to the rest of his furry family, parading them across the floor and out of the room as if his job here was done. And I guess it was. Moses had been the sign I'd looked for. I simply hadn't been expecting a four-legged one, or I would've recognized it sooner. Fine sleuth I was turning out to be.

Noises I couldn't identify came from another part of the house. With such a vast floor plan, the rooms seemed to stretch endlessly. A shiver rippled along my spine at the possibility someone could be somewhere inside. Not a pleasant thought. My breath tight in my throat, I slowly swept the beam of my handy-dandy pocket flashlight up, down, and all around as I walked. I wasn't sure what to look for, but if I could trust a four-legged tour guide to bring me this far safely, I figured there had to be a reason. I was ready for anything as long as it helped me find Poppy Rose's killer.

A generous-sized utility room contained a large, front-loading washer and matching dryer on one wall with an area of coat hooks and a double-door storage closet on the opposite wall. Obviously meant for use as a combination service entrance and laundry room, the room's glass-paned French doors separated it from a fabulous gourmet kitchen. Even a non-cook like me watched enough TV cooking shows to know the high-end, stainless steel appliances would thrill any professional chef.

Since time was short, I did a quick walk-through of the kitchen. My first objective was to find Poppy Rose's bedroom. I mean, wouldn't that be the logical place for the cops to begin their search for clues? I would explore the kitchen more thoroughly on the way out.

The focal point of the front foyer was the massive circular staircase leading to the second floor. Its unique, custom-made bannister of hand-carved poppies was a creative masterpiece that must've cost a fortune. Poppy Rose certainly spared no expense on the furnishings. Just off the foyer was the massive living room and formal dining room decorated as if Poppy had shopped at Tacky in Pink and bought two of everything. My eyes would be bleeding pink if I wasn't careful where I looked. My hand drifted along over the bannister carvings as I climbed.

Expecting more of the same décor on the second floor, I wasn't disappointed. I swept the landing with my flashlight beam and stopped at a large pink and white hydrangea bush blossoming out of a white porcelain urn at the end of the hallway. Out of curiosity, I touched the enormous blooms. Silk, just as I suspected.

I kept the flashlight beam moving as I passed an assortment of odd-shaped wooden and glass-topped tables holding imported knick-knacks of every size and composition. There were enough cobweb-catchers to keep two maids busy with feather dusters or whatever they used on such collectables.

Me, I only needed a rag and a squirt of whatever brand of cleaning spray was on sale at the Dollar'n'Dime store to dust my furniture, and even then it was a hit or miss effort. *Minimal* was my decorating theme. Poppy's choice of décor had definitely been *More is Bettah*, bless her heart.

The first room to my left was the generous-sized master bedroom and en suite. I adjusted my eyes to the dark and slowly moved the beam of my trusty flashlight across the room. Two tall, sheer-curtained windows flanked a four-poster bed with a blush-pink ruffled canopy. A pale glow from the corner street light filtered through the windows, casting pinkish shadow puppets on the wall. I knew Poppy Rose had a thing for the color pink, but lordy sakes, the entire room was a Pepto-Bismol nightmare. Fifty Shades of Flamingo Pink, minus the flamingos. Uh-huh.

Since there wasn't a shred of physical evidence that Parvis had ever shared the room, not even a pair of men's shoes, it was clear the change over to the feminine decor had been done after the poor man's demise. Any male with active testosterone would suffocate on this much sweetness. And that brought me to the matter of Parvis' death and Miss Nettie's implication that the cause of it wasn't at all natural. Did Chief Jackson believe there could be a connection between the two deaths? With so much money at stake and no known heirs, even a layman with half an imagination could come up with a motive or two for the crime.

My sandaled feet sunk into the plush, pink carpeting with each step I took through the room. I swung the flashlight beam across the ornate vanity, finding nothing but exotic designer perfumes and more of Poppy Rose's tacky collectables. Not being a hoarder of anything except bad luck, I wouldn't know the value of her shiny trinkets if it jumped up and smacked me in the face with a spreadsheet. But I was positive the baubles weren't to my liking.

The temptation to look inside the tall, mahogany armoire tugged at my conscience something fierce. Hey, I already risked being charged with breaking and entering simply by being inside the place. Ignoring the armoire wouldn't make matters any worse. Still, if I wanted to get to the bottom of the mystery and absolve myself of the crime—well, everyone knows a woman's gotta do . . . blah, blah, blah.

With the flashlight tucked under my arm, I used both hands to pull open the armoire's double doors. Like a fridge, the closet light came on automatically when the doors opened. WHAAA!! I shielded my eyes from instant blindness. The intense, blue-white beam of light from a spotlight the size of a basketball zapped me. My little flashlight fell to the floor with a muffled thump, protected from shattering by the plush carpet.

I blinked a couple of times to focus my eyes, which by now had irises the size of a dime, grabbed the flashlight, and began checking out the garments hanging haphazardly from a metal rod. The limited space held mostly matching designer slacks and tops plus a few sequined gowns of various lengths. All shades pink, of course. Nothing belonging to Parvis. I closed the armoire and swept the flashlight beam around the room one more time. Surely, there had to be a bigger walk-in closet with a dressing area somewhere. The bedroom was as large as my entire house.

I moved through the peppermint maze, careful not to knock over any of the glass doo-dads while I poked around. Nothing the least bit suspicious caught my attention, no ransom notes with threats of any kind, no incriminating photos of a secret affair, nothing to hint at why someone might want to kill Poppy Rose. Not even the dresser drawer filled with silky, pale, barely there lingerie.

I hurried into the en suite bathroom and Bingo! A bathroom to die for, no pun intended. As spacious as the master bedroom, this room housed a walk-in closet with rotating hangers on two sides of the room that reminded me of the ones at the dry cleaners. There was also a mirrored dressing area complete with a chaise lounge and a mini-bar. The place was big enough to throw a party for a crowd and have room to spare.

I pushed the button to start the revolving track of hangers. Wow! What knock-out-gorgeous clothes, but there were way more than one person needed or could wear in a year. Some of the garments looked like they'd never been worn. Pink wasn't my color, but I wouldn't turn down a chance to own a few of the outfits with designer labels. I peeked at the tag. Size Zero. Huh? Oh well, they really weren't my style. And where in the world would I wear such fancy duds, anyway? Cleaning up puppy poop at Doc's clinic?

I moved into the bathroom area, shining the flashlight on the rosy marble fixtures tastefully separated from the walk-in closet by a privacy wall covered with flocked wallpaper in shades of cherry blossom and rose hues. I began to see a cotton-candy-colored theme here. My brain began to overload.

The main feature in the room had to be the biggest bathtub I'd ever seen. All you needed was a cabana boy and you could hold a heck of a pool party in that thing. Who needs something as big as that unless . . . ? Remembering the stash of sensuous underwear I'd seen, I wondered if Poppy Rose had a private side of her life she kept hidden from the community. My suspicions were crazy, and I didn't want to believe them, but I had been gone from Ruby Springs for a mighty long time. Poppy Rose had changed, and so had I.

I did my best not to criticize the extravagant use of gilded trim on the double vanity, but honestly, rose-tinted marble sinks and toilets are hard to ignore. The blush-colored toilet paper made me grin, but when I saw the candy-pink bidet, I clapped my hand over my mouth to keep from laughing out loud. Somehow bidets in rural West Texas didn't quite fit the image most folks have of the Lone Star State. Outhouses, maybe, but bidets?

Still chuckling, I checked the contents of the vanity drawers. Nothing in them but the usual dental products, along with enough high-end makeup to paint the faces of a half-dozen rodeo clowns. Assorted face creams by the quart took up a whole drawer built to accommodate their size. From the amount of expensive products I found, Poppy Rose's makeover was a high-maintenance, forever kind of project.

I opened the door of the large cabinet on the wall next to the large vanity mirror. Nothing unusual there except the amount of hair products it held. What a waste. All those gels and sprays could've kept her big Texas hair immobile for weeks.

Checking the shower was creepier than I'd expected. I crossed my fingers and hoped there wouldn't be another body lurking behind the beveled glass doors, and sighed with relief when there was nothing but shiny, pink-and-white tiles and more of the gilded fixtures.

Disappointed at finding no significant evidence leading to Poppy's killer, I still held out hope of discovering something as I thoroughly searched each of the other three bedrooms before going back downstairs. Surprisingly, or maybe not, Poppy Rose hadn't shared the pink theme in the other rooms.

The remaining three bedrooms shouted TEXAS in patriotic red, white, and blue and were as different from the rest of the plantation house style as sic 'em from c'mere. Lone Star flags hung from corner flagpoles in each suite, and wall shelves held tiny ceramic bales of cotton, silver miniature oil wells and pump jacks, as well as assorted sizes of ceramic and glass models of the Alamo. Silk arrangements of bluebonnets in vases of various sizes and designs were everywhere—on tables, wall shelves, and dresser tops. And longhorns, big ones, little ones, brass ones, glass ones.

As if she'd been afraid of not having enough reminders of her home state, Poppy Rose also had paintings of Longhorn cattle, cowboys, and horses along the walls of one bedroom that I guessed belonged to Parvis because of the adjoining study. The Texas-themed room had a good-size sitting area with two chairs covered in faux cowhide on either side of an oval table made from mesquite wood.

The lamps on the tables had once been old oil lanterns. I was fascinated by the stone fireplace and the photos on the mantle, especially the unexpected framed one of Poke, Parvis, and Wilbur taken on the front steps of the verandah. I did a quick check of the desk to see if any more interesting photos turned up, but found nothing more.

Curious to see the rest, I made my way to the en suite bathroom with its saddle-shaped toilet seats and mounted racks of horns on the wall next to the shower and above the uniquely-shaped urinal. Definitely a man's room, but, strangely, I sensed a floral scent. A chill raced through me.

Not at all comfortable in the shadows of the male facility, and anxious now to get out of there, I turned and tripped over a metal tool box left open on the floor by the vanity. Whoever had been fixing pipes under the sink hadn't bothered to finish the job. The loud clatter of tools scattered echoed through the vastness of the empty house. A sound much like a door opening startled me. I scooted downstairs, fearing I might have tripped an alarm that would bring the entire police in search of a burglar and finding me.

I hurried through the hallway and into the opulent kitchen. Something hard and heavy smacked the back of my head. Stars twinkled and bells rang. After that, I didn't remember diddly.

Chapter Fourteen

Fuzzy. Everything is fuzzy, and oooh, my head hurts. Someone's calling my name and shaking my shoulder. Stop that!

I tried to slap the hand away, but my arms were too heavy to move. Groaning, I peeked out from beneath heavy eyelids. *Wow! This dream's too good to miss.* My eyes closed again. I wanted the dream to continue.

If Joe Camps wants to star in my fantasy, who am I to refuse? If only he'd stop shaking me. Makes my head hurt something fierce.

"Frankie Lou, please look at me." That voice! I know that voice.

A cold, wet cloth pressed against my forehead. My eyes flew open. "Joe! You really are . . . I mean, what are you doing here?" My tongue was suddenly too big for my mouth. I was babbling, and why wouldn't I? This was no fantasy. This was the real deal.

Sprawled on the floor outside the pantry with the bigger-than-life, in-the-flesh Joe Camps kneeling beside me, I couldn't think of a single reason to get up.

"I'm trying to revive you, okay? You were out cold when I found you. What happened here?"

His touch was gentle as he continued to bathe my face with the damp cloth. When he slid an arm behind me to help me sit up my mind went blank. Words escaped me. I simply stared at the crinkles around those melted-chocolate eyes. The way his mouth tilted slightly upward on one side and the faint shadow of stubble hugging his jaw was worth more than a passing glance, too, so I took extra time there, even though the pain in my head pounded relentlessly.

For the second time since Poppy's death, my poor skull had taken a whack. The first time was in Chief Jackson's office, and the company wasn't nearly as good-looking as today's. Obviously, a large part of my common sense leaked out every time my noggin took a hard blow. At this rate, one more time and I'd be plumb empty-headed.

"How . . . how did you get inside this house?" My head might be throbbing, but I still recognized a scary possibility when I saw one. Holy Moley! Was good-looking Joe my attacker? Had he turned to burglary when he couldn't find a job in town? This empty mansion was full of valuables. I shivered. How much did I really know about the man? Panic caught in my throat.

"No problem. I used a key," Joe said, so matter-of-fact I almost believed him. Almost. "So, how'd you get that goose egg back here?" He touched the spot on my head that ached like a sore tooth. "I'll go look for some ice. I can wrap some in this cloth to hold on it."

"No, no. I'm okay," I said, wincing as I gently examined the lump. "I guess I ran into the door when I came out of the pantry." I quickly scanned the room, expecting to see ... oh, I don't know ... his accomplice, perhaps, or a partner in crime? But no one else appeared to be with him, so where did his key come from? I had to know.

"Joe, why do you have a key to Poppy Rose's house? You shouldn't even be here. Don't you know this place is part of an on-going crime investigation?" He didn't look like a burglar. Not that I've ever met one face to face, but hey, I watch those cop shows on television. Still . . .

Joe arched an eyebrow. "Oh? And I suppose you're part of the police crime unit, huh? Are the street cops using bikes now?"

Well, shoot! My bike was outside by the fence. Who else had passed by and seen it? Did Ruby Springs's finest have a night patrol on this side of town? I had a key, too, but only by a twist of fate—and Miss Nettie, of course. No way would I share that information.

"Joe, do the police know you have that key?" I steered the conversation away from me and hoped he didn't fire my question right back, 'cause I didn't have any excuse for being here. At least, none that would keep me out of jail.

"Matter of fact, they don't, Frankie Lou. This key belongs to Gus Mosely, the man I do odd jobs for once in a while. He gave it to me so I could get in and pick up the toolbox. He left it here when he was working on the bathroom, and then the house got locked down after the murder. He just got permission to remove it from the house when his trick knee went out. He asked me to pick it up for him, and I agreed. Not a problem for me. I'll give the key back when I take the toolbox to him."

He fiddled with the wet cloth in his hands like he didn't know what to do with it now. Maybe he was simply having trouble telling me the truth. I didn't like the direction my thoughts were headed. I guess we both looked a little guilty for being here. In an empty house. In the early hours of the morning. Oh, yeah, not good.

With Joe's help, I stood, waiting for my wobbly legs to steady a little before testing them. Waking up with Joe's face hovering over mine pretty much sent any logical brain activity into hiding. Sticking around much longer would only lead to trouble. Something about good-looking, broad-shouldered men wearing plaid shirts and snug jeans messed with the sensible side of my brain, making me forget important stuff like how long he'd been in jail or the details of his acquittal.

I should leave, but with my arms half-numb and my legs weak as wet noodles, I seriously doubted my ability to move. Besides, I had a few more questions for Mr. Hunky Joe Camps to answer while I waited for the blood to do a rerun through my limp limbs.

"Joe, how did Gus happen to have a key to the Fremont place?"

He grew quiet, as if he was considering what I'd asked. "He takes care of the grounds here and some other places. You know, mowing lawns, stuff like that. Keeps the yards looking neat and tidy. A handyman."

Handyman, huh! I wasn't buying that. "Why would he need a house key if he only did yard work?"

"Oh, he does more than cut grass. He repairs other things inside the house, too, like broken door handles, clogged drains, leaky faucets. That's what he'd been doing when he forgot his toolbox. If it's broken, most likely he can repair it. Odd jobs, he calls 'em, but some of them are pretty tricky."

Okay, that sounded almost like a legitimate reason, but I couldn't shake the suspicion still bothering me. "Why on earth did he need his toolbox so early today? I can't imagine anyone wanting home repair done before breakfast, for crying out loud."

"Figured I'd pick it up before I got Wesley off to school. I owed him a favor."

"A favor?"

"Yeah. Yesterday Gus offered me part-time work helping him when he gets real busy. He was the only person in town willing to take a chance on an ex-con. I wanted to show my appreciation, that's all. I'll tackle any kind of job, Frankie Lou. I'm not afraid of hard work."

"I'm sure you're not, Joe. I didn't mean to insinuate otherwise. Working any sort of job is admirable." Sheesh! How did my foot get in my mouth? "You know, Miss Nettie always has something around her house that needs fixing. I'll be sure to let her know you're working for Gus now. And if you ever take up car repairs, I've got a van that could use a lot of help."

"I know a fair amount about what's under the hood of a car. Tell you what," Joe said, "I'll stop by one evening and take a look at yours.

Right now, I need to grab Gus's toolbox. Then I'll walk you and your bike home when you feel ready to leave."

I wasn't sure how I felt about that, but he handed me the still-damp cloth and left the room before I could protest.

I needed time to sort out the disturbing thoughts that were giving me the headache of the century. The shock of meeting Joe again under such puzzling circumstances made me suspicious of his story about Gus and the toolbox. Still, he'd been genuinely concerned about my injury. He'd even tried to revive me with that cold cloth on my forehead. He was right about the location of the bump on my head, too. Someone had ambushed me from behind and whacked me a good one, but who? And where had the guilty party come from? Were they hiding inside when I came in?

At first, it was easy for the logical side of my brain to cast Joe as the culprit. He had a key and his arrival had been conveniently well-timed. But his explanation made sense.

Sounds of mewing kittens coming from the other part of the house alerted me of Joe's return. Moses came sashaying into the room proudly leading the way in front of Joe. Behind them, the quartet of fuzzy fur babies tumbled and rolled across the floor, mewing happily. Mrs. Moses was nowhere to be seen. Probably enjoying a break from her energetic brood. Couldn't blame her.

"Matthew, Mark, Luke, and John," I said, observing the parade of tiny kitties.

Joe inclined his head and gave me a puzzled look. "Are you sure they're all boys?"

"No, but they could be. Their father's Moses, and those were the first biblical ones that popped into my head. Aren't they adorable?"

"The names or the kittens?" Joe teased.

"Kittens, silly."

"Well, kittens are cute, but they grow up to be cats. Give me a dog any day."

"Puppies grow up to be dogs," I countered, picking up a white ball of fluff to cuddle.

"Yeah," Joe said, "but dogs don't *meow*."

Arguing kittens versus puppies right then was the last thing I wanted to do. There were so many other, more important matters on my mind. My aching head was one of them. I put the kitten on the floor and felt the lump on the back of my head.

"Wow! That was one humdinger of a wallop."

Joe frowned. "Do you remember hitting the back of your head on the floor when you fell?"

"I didn't fall, Joe. I'm pretty sure I tangled with a cabinet door."

"Were you walking backwards? The bump's on the back of your head. Seriously, Frankie Lou, you need to call the police about this. Got your cell phone handy?"

"Oh, uh, no. Battery's dead," I said, proud of my quick thinking.

"Too bad. I don't have a phone, either," he said.

I leaned against the wall to keep from sliding to the floor. "What time is it, anyway? Did you happen to see anyone lurking inside the house while you were here or coming out? Anyone on the street?"

"Nope. Almost 6 a.m. I saw a—"

"Six a.m.? It can't be!" I'd been gone for—I couldn't calculate the missing hours—well, way too long, I know. "Momma will be frantic, and Betsy has to get to school." The more I thought about my foolish decision to come over here, the more my head pounded. When would I learn to think ahead? "What time did you get here, Joe?"

"About fifteen minutes ago. I saw you first thing when I walked into the back entry. You were lying on the kitchen floor so still I thought you were dead. Scared the bejeebers out of me, too, until I heard you moan. I've been trying to wake you up ever since then."

"I'm glad you came along when you did. Are you sure you didn't see anyone coming out of the house when you got here?"

"Nope. All I saw was a bike lying in the grass outside the fence, but it was pretty far away from the gate. I didn't think much about it at the time." He studied me with such intense concentration I felt warm all over. "You look mighty pale. Want me to get another cold cloth for your head?"

"No, no, no! I'm okay. I'll take something for my headache when I get home and can lie down for a while. I can't believe I was knocked out for so long. I'm surprised Momma hasn't been out looking for me. She usually wakes up early. What a mess. I'd better get started biking home."

"So that's your bike out there? You're in no shape to ride it now. Besides, it's better if you stay awake after a hit on the head like that. You could have a concussion. Maybe you ought to go to ER or the walk-in clinic."

"That's farther away than my house. I'd never make it." I didn't want to go anywhere but home to bed, and I definitely didn't want the police coming here asking questions. No way! Charging me with breaking into Poppy Rose's house would totally make Detective Hardy's day and the chief's, too. I should think Joe wouldn't want to be found here, either, but he didn't seem too worried, and that puzzled me.

He moved inside my comfort zone and placed a restraining hand lightly on my arm. "I've got the toolbox now. If you feel ready to leave, I'll walk you and your bike home. You aren't steady enough to ride, and I'd feel responsible if you had an accident."

I backed away. "That's really not necessary, Joe, but thanks for the first-aid. I'm feeling much better now. And I promise to take a pain pill when I get home." *Two, if Momma is waiting for me.*

My head pounded, and I was sweaty and shaky, but I still had one or two working brain cells. Having Joe Camps accompany me home wasn't going to happen. He'd probably insist I call the cops and stick around until they arrived so he could add his comments to the story. I had to think of some excuse to get rid of him by the time we reached the street.

When we approached the big gate I expected Joe to get out his key. When he didn't, I asked about it. "Aren't you going to use a key?"

"Don't need one to get out. Laser beam." He pointed to the tiny light on the inside of the brick wall and flashed a smug grin.

"Oh, sure, I knew that. Just wondered if you did," I said, expecting bumps to appear on my tongue for that white lie. Apparently, leaving the estate wasn't a problem. Getting in was. I'd worried for no reason.

Once outside the gate, Joe stopped to set the toolbox down and pulled a bottle of water from his backpack. "Here, I should've given you some of this sooner. You need to hydrate. You look like you're about to keel over." With a twist, he removed the top and handed me the bottle. "By the way, you never told me why you were in the Fremont house."

Wasn't going to, either. I took a swig of water and wiped the back of my hand across my mouth. "Thanks. I hadn't realized I was so thirsty."

I lifted the bottle to take another drink as a dark sedan glided by, stopped suddenly a few feet ahead of us, and, in the time it took me to swallow, had backed up and squealed to a stop alongside of us with its engine idling.

Inside my chest, my heart did major flip-flops. I didn't recognize the car. Was this a drive-by shooting? Perspiration dampened my forehead and beaded on my upper lip. A hard fist of anxiety knotted in my belly. None of these sensations had anything to do with the steamy Texas morning, either.

I looked at Joe. His lips were pressed firmly together. His body tense, on alert. Was there a connection between Joe and the strange car? All sorts of scenarios ran rampant through my mind. After all, how much did I really know about him? Following my intuition hadn't worked out too well with my ex.

I whispered his name. "Joe?"

"It's okay," he said quietly. "I'm probably the one they want. Let me do the talking."

They? Who the heck were they? Were we about to be offed by a crime boss or worse? *God, are you there? We could use a little help down here. Please?*

The vehicle's darkened, curb-side window slid down with a whisper, and I heard my name called out. Cold fear clogged my throat. Now I knew who *they* were.

Detective Hardy rode shotgun with Chief Jackson behind the wheel. But the kicker of this not-to-be-believed fiasco was the face glaring at me through the lowered back seat window. I was busted by my own momma, bless her floral, polyester heart.

CRUNCHED INTO the back seat of the chief's car with Momma, I had to ride back to the police station while Joe followed on my bike. Momma talked the entire time about how I'd been gone all night and how I'd caused so much trouble by not leaving her a note explaining where I'd gone and how I was setting a bad example for Betsy. By the time we finally got back to the police station, my jaw ached from clenching it hard so I wouldn't scream. I envied Joe his quiet bike ride.

Not by choice, Chief Jackson's office was becoming a familiar destination. Joe and I sat in front of the chief's desk while Momma fretted and stewed behind me on a folding chair well out of my peripheral vision. The detective stood near the desk flipping through his neon orange notebook.

Chief Jackson didn't look happy. Well, big whoopee, neither was I, and I was pretty sure Joe felt the same. Maybe worse. We weren't there for a party.

We'd been waiting twenty minutes for Gus Mosely to call back after the chief gave Joe permission to use the phone. The handyman was Joe's alibi, not mine. I didn't have one. Didn't have a clue how I was going to get one, either. I couldn't, and wouldn't, incriminate Miss Nettie or the church, even if she had given me the key. I was the trespasser on the Fremont property. *It's me, Frankie Lou, again. Forgive my trespasses, Lord.*

Behind me, Momma gave orders like a hard-boiled drill sergeant. "Chief, I insist you release Frances Louise into my custody. I'll make certain this sort of thing doesn't happen again."

"I'm not twelve, Momma." I didn't turn around for fear I'd act like I was and say something I'd regret. I knew how she'd react without looking at her. "I'm quite capable of handling my own problems."

Momma *tsk-tsk'd* like always. "You've yet to convince your father and me of that, Frances Louise."

I was about to tell her I'd been aware of that fact for several years when Chief Jackson called a time-out on us.

"Ladies, please refrain from any further quarreling until Detective Hardy and I review the statements from Miz McMasters and Mr. Camps. Officer Townsend will be arriving shortly with Mr. Mosely." No sooner said than the pair arrived.

Gus hobbled into the room with the help of a cane and Officer Townsend, who seated him next to Joe. The handyman's appearance left no doubt he'd been asleep when Joe had called him. His rumpled work shirt and jeans were clean, but he hadn't shaved, and he had a major case of bed head. Was he married? I'd ask Joe later.

After the two exchanged howdys, Gus leaned around Joe and nodded to me, which was a little surprising, since I barely knew the man. Behind us, Momma scooted her chair closer to the front. No surprise there. She hated being behind anyone.

Detective Hardy remained standing. Chief Jackson cleared his throat. Both men's expressions were grim and a mighty long way from friendly.

Big whoopee! Let the games begin.

The chief nodded to Hardy. "Detective Hardy, why don't you start?"

Hardy consulted his notes and addressed Joe. "Let me get this straight, Mr. Camp. You went inside the Fremont place and found Miz McMasters out cold on the floor near the back entrance, right?"

"That's correct," Joe said. "I grabbed a clean towel from the pantry, got it wet at the kitchen sink, and wiped her face. Thought it would help wake her up. From the size of the knot on the back of her head, someone whacked her pretty hard."

"What makes you think someone attacked her, Mr. Camps? Did you see or hear anyone else in the house? Did you find any type of weapon?" Detective Hardy reviewed his notes again. "Miz McMasters claims she bumped into a pantry door."

Joe shook his head. "Not possible, Detective. She's got a goose egg on the back of her head the size of a baseball. If she ran into the door, the bump would be on her forehead."

"Smart observation. Remind me again, Mr. Camps, how you came to have a key to that house and why you were there," the detective continued.

Gus Mosely stood up and shook his fist at Hardy. "He come by it rightly 'cause I give it to him!"

"Thank you, Mr. Mosely. If you'll have a seat, we'll get to you next," Chief Jackson said, poker-faced as a corpse.

Momma fidgeted behind me and muttered under her breath. Keeping quiet wasn't easy for my formerly demure Momma. I wish I knew what had come over her since she and Daddy moved to Florida.

By the time Detective Hardy and Chief Jackson finished interviewing Joe, and Gus had explained about the toolbox to their satisfaction, I was fighting to stay awake. A cup of Miss Nettie's coffee would have been welcome right about now, but then I'd have to make a trip to the ladies' room. If I didn't want to miss anything, I'd have to forget coffee and try harder to pay attention.

"Mr. Mosely, I strongly advise you not to give that key to anyone again without checking with the attorney handling the Fremont affairs. You're free to go now and thank you for cooperating. One of the officers will take you home."

After Gus was escorted from the room, the two lawmen turned their attention to the rest of us. I was relieved that Joe's actions had been validated by Gus's statement, but didn't feel confident about my own fate.

"Mr. Camps," the Chief said looking straight at Joe, "we'd like you and Miz McMasters to stay a little longer. Detective Hardy and I have a few more questions for both of you." Joe never blinked, just nodded, and I marveled at his calmness.

Momma popped up from her chair, hands fisted on her grass-green and yellow floral polyester-clad hips. She must've slept in her clothes or dressed faster than she usually did. Even her hairdo was perfect. "Chief Jackson, how long do you intend to hold us here like common criminals?"

"Until we get the answers we need, Miz Birmingham, ma'am."

I looked at Joe. "This could take a while," I whispered.

"You have no idea," he muttered under his breath.

Chapter Fifteen

Miss Nettie marched into the Chief's office with Betsy in tow. Momma had asked her to come over and stay with Betsy while she went looking for me. Now Miss Nettie was in a tizzy—ready to leave on the bus tour with the Library Ladies. I'd forgotten all about her plans until she showed up wearing the periwinkle blue silk frock she reserved for special occasions. No wonder she was in such a hurry. The bus was leaving at seven-forty-five.

Chief Jackson rose when she entered the room. "Miss Nettie, what brings you here so early this mornin'?" He smiled at her like we were all there to have a tea party instead of an interrogation. *Pffit!* I didn't like the man much after I realized he didn't believe a word I'd said at any of my questionings. I knew he wanted to nail me as the guilty party so he could close the case, but I wasn't giving in yet. I wanted to know who the real bad guy was—the person who killed Poppy Rose.

Miss Nettie leaned over Chief Jackson's desk, got right in his face, and wasted no time telling him what was on her mind.

"Now you listen to me, Noah Jackson. This child needs her momma to come home right now." She pointed at Betsy, who was sound asleep in a chair. Then she poked the chief in the chest. "I'm a'going on that bus tour in forty-five minutes, and Betsy needs to get to school pretty soon. You better put an end to this questioning business right now so Frankie Lou can come take care of her, you hear me?"

Before the chief had time to blink, Miss Nettie rounded the desk, and her tight little fist connected with his broad shoulder hard enough to spin him around in his squeaky chair.

Caught off guard, the chief went over backward. For such a small woman, she sure packed a hefty wallop when she got all fired up.

Lord deliver us! We're all going to jail. I pulled Betsy to my side and hugged her tight. What would she think of me now? Luckily, she yawned and kept sleeping.

Detective Hardy politely restrained my feisty neighbor with a firm hold on her arm. Joe and I stayed out of the way. The chief got to his feet. Clutching his shoulder on the way out of the room, he passed Miss Nettie and paused briefly to speak to her.

"I assure you, Miss Nettie, the matter will be taken care of right away. Next time, please call and ask for help. It'll be much easier on everyone." He turned to the rest of us still in our seats, his grim face flushed. "Now, if y'all will excuse me for a minute . . ."

Chief Jackson left the room, his face screwed up in pain. The rest of us stared after him, too stunned to speak.

Detective Hardy coughed politely to break the silence. "Recovering from shoulder surgery," he murmured. He still held Miss Nettie's arm, although not as tightly as he had right to after she'd physically delivered her message to the Chief.

Miss Nettie shrugged. "Oops!"

"Officer Townsend is off duty now, but Officer Quigley will see that you're all driven home," Hardy said. "He'll take you right to the tour bus first, Miss Nettie. You won't miss the trip. There are no charges against any of you, but the chief and I may have more questions later, so please be available and don't leave town." He turned to Joe. "Mr. Camps, that especially means you."

"Well, I declare," Miss Nettie sputtered. "All that fuss over a sore shoulder? I'm still going on that bus tour, detective, and I don't need the police to take me. How would that look, showing up in a police cruiser? You can tell the chief 'Thanks but no thanks.' *Humph!* Can't even handle a little poke. What a weenie." She marched past Hardy and another officer. Neither man tried to stop her. I wasn't surprised.

"I'll be along in a minute," I said. I figured Momma and Miss Nettie, being adults and all, could fend for themselves. I had a feeling Miss Nettie wouldn't refuse the ride and risk being late. I had one more thing I wanted to do before I left the police station. With Betsy still sleeping in a chair, bundled in a light blanket, I approached Detective Hardy.

"Would there be any reason for Poke deHaven or anyone else to have been at the Fremont estate last night?"

I was so focused on hearing the detective's response I didn't notice Joe slipping up beside me. His raspy whisper took me by surprise.

"What are you doing, Frankie Lou? Trying to get arrested?"

I whispered back fiercely, "No, but this might be—"

Detective Hardy eyed us both with a look of suspicion. "Do you have something more to say, Miz McMasters? Something about what went on at the Fremont house?"

I swallowed my fear and forged ahead. "I'm not sure, but when I was, uh, upstairs I smelled a very faint scent similar to the fragrance Divinity Pettibone wears and so does her sister, Delilah, who was at Poppy's service at the cemetery. I thought perhaps one of them had been inside the house."

"You went upstairs in the empty house? For what reason? And before you answer, Miz McMasters, let me assure you that no one had official permission to be in that house until Mr. Hadley escorted the Probate folks through. No one!"

Rats! My chances now of finding Poppy Rose's killer were *kaput*. If I couldn't come up with a believable excuse, I might as well admit defeat and pay the consequences. And I didn't have a clue how to get out of this present predicament. I brushed away the stray cat hairs from Moses and his family clinging to my capris and pondered my future with a heavy heart. Wait a minute! Cat hair? Moses? *Bazinga!* I found my alibi.

"Yes, of course, I'll be happy to explain," I said, false confidence appearing out of nowhere, a welcome surprise. "I was out looking for Miss Nettie's cat, Moses. You see, when Moses wasn't at her house when we got back from our little 'visit' with you, she got worried. I decided to ride around on my bike and see if I could find him."

Suddenly Betsy was beside me. "Miss Nettie didn't say anything to Grammy about Moses being lost, Momma." She nudged me sleepily. "You were gone when we got up. Grammy didn't know where you were and was worried about you. Why didn't you leave us a note?"

Detective Hardy jumped right on that bit of information, but I couldn't blame Betsy. "So you left home without telling anyone? If you left after you took Miss Nettie home, how do you explain being inside the house until this morning? Was Mr. Camps with you all that time?"

My heart sunk. I didn't have time to sync the past few hours in my story, and now it sounded as if Joe and I had spent the night in the Fremont place, in spite of his alibi from Gus. I hadn't mentioned that I had a key, either, and wasn't going to. Guilt is a bitter pill to swallow. Crow doesn't taste so good, either. No matter how I phrased my alibi, I came up looking guilty. And I wasn't! But, if I told the truth now it would implicate Miss Nettie, and I would never do that. If ever I needed Divine help, now was the perfect time for a miracle.

Joe spoke. "I let Frankie Lou inside the house. With my key." In an instant, my knight in non-shiny denim jeans and plaid shirt was covering for me. Joe slid a sideways glance at me with those sexy, dark eyes. Was that a wink? A delicious tingle of something I couldn't identify danced beneath the surface of my skin. Talk about a miracle. *Wowza!* I held my breath, wondering what was brewing behind those teasing eyes. A knot of anxiety tightened in my chest.

But the good detective wasn't interested in my inner thoughts, thank goodness. He was zeroed in on what Joe had just told him. Not so thankful about that.

"Hold on a minute, Mr. Camps," Hardy said. "You didn't mention this when Chief Jackson questioned you a few minutes ago. I'd like to hear what else you have to say."

Joe shifted his weight so my shoulder rested against his, supporting me in more ways than one. Funny, how that little bit of reassurance bolstered my confidence.

"It's like this, Detective," Joe began in that slow Texas drawl that had my toes curling and my heart doing jumping jacks. "I was walking along, minding my business on my way to the Fremont place, when I saw Frankie Lou on her bike. Naturally, I asked her why she was out riding so early. She told me about the lost cat, so I offered to help her look for him. We were going the same direction, anyhow." He kept his tone casual-like. I wondered how he could be so calm. Wasn't he afraid he'd go back to jail?

"We were at the gate to the estate," he continued, "when old Moses came shootin' out from behind a bush and ran around to the back of the house. I told Frankie Lou she might as well come with me and take a look around while I collected Gus's toolbox, and that's what she did. Sure enough, Moses was inside with a passel of kittens. He wasn't lost, just visiting. I had access to the front gate and the house from Gus, like he told you. Getting in wasn't a problem."

Joe's quick-thinking storytelling just saved my life.

"Yes, yes, that's what we did," I said, playing along, but feeling a little like I was flying blind.

Detective Hardy rubbed his chin. After a minute, he pointed to the chairs we'd just vacated. "Well now, I think you folks better sit back down, while I see if Chief Jackson's able to come back in here and hear this new development."

Betsy fidgeted at my side. "Momma, can I wait in the other room with Grammy and Miss Nettie?"

"Of course you can, sweetie." No sense subjecting her to any further discomfort.

Like any normal twelve-year-old, she darted out of the room before I could change my mind.

"I'll have the women and little girl escorted safely home now," the detective told us.

There was nothing for us to do but agree. When Hardy opened the door, I heard Momma sputtering her disapproval as she, Miss Nettie and Betsy were escorted out of the building. I didn't look forward to a confrontation with her when I got home. I went back to my chair, more worried than ever.

Joe sat next to me and slid his arm across the back of my chair like he'd been doing it for years. "Thanks for going along with my story."

I laughed, surprisingly comfortable having his arm in close proximity to my shoulders. Very comfortable, indeed. "I'm the one who should be thanking you for your quick thinking," I said, hoping he hadn't heard the hitch in my voice.

"No problem," he said. "Glad to help. I owed you one, remember?" He winked, and right then, I swear his plaid shirt glowed like a knight's shiniest armor. Seriously.

WE DIDN'T HURRY on the way home, but we didn't rush, either. Joe walked beside me, pushing my bike along the sidewalk, the toolbox balanced on the handle bars. Morning traffic was beginning to flow in all directions as the streets filled with people on their way to work.

"I could've ridden my bike home by myself," I said for the second or third time. "You didn't have to come with me."

"Oh, I don't doubt you can take care of yourself, Frankie Lou, but I wanted to see for myself that you got home safely. Thanks for tolerating my stubbornness, okay?"

"Okay. I do appreciate it, Joe. Really. I'm so sorry I got you involved in this whole mess."

"Aw, it'll all work out. The chief and Detective Hardy will find who they're looking for. It might take a while, though. Like they said, you have to let them do their work. Remember, you've got The Joyful Noise gang and their rehearsals to think about. They need you right now. Just holler, and I'll be happy help out anytime."

"You're right, I know. And I appreciate your offer to help, Joe. I want to get the case solved as quickly as possible so my life can get back to normal, but it feels like the police are deliberately dragging their feet with the investigation. Guess I'm too impatient."

We reached my house, and I waited by the front door while Joe wheeled my bike up the driveway and gave the stand a kick. I was so exhausted mentally and physically from the intensive questioning, all I wanted to do was sleep for a hundred hours. Hopefully, Momma had made certain Betsy got to school on time. I dreaded face time with her until I'd had food and sleep, in that order.

"Don't worry too much about the investigation," Joe said on his way up the porch steps. He looked me straight on. "The chief and Detective Hardy have a good handle on the case." He laid his hand on my arm, barely touching, but a comfort nonetheless. "Remember, I've got your back. Now get some sleep. I'll call you later."

I longed for a nap but was reluctant to say goodbye. "Let me drive you home, Joe. After all, you've done a lot of walking and bike riding this morning. C'mon, the van's in the garage."

He hesitated, but I persisted. "You can listen to the noisy engine then. Please?"

Joe looked thoughtful a moment, then he smiled. "Okay, I guess I could do that. Let me grab the toolbox."

"I'll go in and grab my keys while you do that," I said and hurried into the house.

A note from Momma was propped up by a water glass on the kitchen table. She'd taken Betsy to school and was meeting her friends for coffee in town. *Yes!* I did a fist pump in the air on my way to the bathroom for a necessary visit. Hands washed, a quick glance in mirror rated a big *Phooey!* I grabbed a ribbon off the vanity and smoothed my hair into a ponytail. Deciding no amount of makeup would turn me from a pumpkin into Cinderella, I grabbed my driver's license and car keys and dashed back to the garage. Joe was leaning against the van's fender waiting patiently. He pushed away when he saw me and hurried to open the driver's door for me. His gentlemanly gesture was such a surprise I almost forgot to say thank you. Wowza! Great looking and totes manners, too.

I got in, and he closed the door. I buckled up, smiling inwardly as he slid in and buckled up, too. When I turned on the key, the engine made a painful grinding noise and cut out with a whine. I tried two more times and got the same results.

"That doesn't sound good," Joe said.

I checked the gauge and shook my head. "I'm not out of gas. Half a tank left." Well, shoot. Now what?

"An empty gas tank wouldn't cause that sound." He got out and lifted the hood. After a minute, he hollered, "Try again."

I did. Same noise only louder.

"Turn it off." He closed the hood and approached my side of the van. "Wesley said the kids were coming here tonight for an extra rehearsal. I'll come back this evening after the kids finish practicing and see if I can get it started for you. I'll just take out the tools I need for the fix-it job I have to do and leave the box here. Gus needs help dismantling the drain in the baptistery. That way I won't have to lug the heavy thing back and forth, if that's okay with you."

"Sure, that's fine. What's wrong with the drain?"

He opened the door for me. "Detective Hardy hired him to take it apart. Apparently he thought it might be clogged."

"Oh," I said, getting out and following him.

He grabbed the tools he needed, then carried the tool box to the back of the single-car garage and set it down in the corner. "You won't forget to lock your service door when I leave, will you?"

"Not a chance. The toolbox will be safe right there until you come back for it."

I walked out of the garage with him and said goodbye. "I'll see you later tonight."

"Count on it," he said and set off whistling. I watched him walk away, already anticipating seeing him again tonight. "Way to go, ol' girl." I gave Minnie-Van a grateful pat on her fender and went inside. Some days bad happenings turn into good things.

TOO WOUND UP to stay at home like Joe suggested, I took a quick shower and showed up for work by noon.

The afternoon flew by, as Doc had a full schedule, but I managed to find time, in-between cleaning up after sick, barfing puppies and consoling a worried cat owner, for worrying about the million-and-one things I needed to accomplish before the fundraiser concert. I fretted about the slow-moving police investigation into Poppy's death and pondered over the possibilities.

Was it only kidnapping gone wrong or a robbery at the wrong place and the wrong time? Neither of those answers satisfied me. *Follow the money*—I'd heard that phrase once on a cop show. Who would inherit the Fremont money now? What would the probate investigation find? What had Poke sneaking around the estate instead of knocking on the front door of his daughter's home?

Oddly enough, the other day I'd taken the long way to work and walked along Blessing Street. I passed the church as the crime unit swarmed over the parking lot and around the dumpster while the big garbage truck waited impatiently to exchange the full container for an empty one. I'd told Chief Jackson my findings about the blood. Maybe he'd taken them seriously. I prayed they'd find a solution—and the real killer—soon.

Tonight though, The Joyful Noise was coming over to get one extra practice in before the big fundraiser concert on the church lawn, and I had plenty to do after I got home from work. Kids were always hungry, and, unfortunately, my reserve stash of snacks was pitifully low. Miss Nettie was on her bus tour and wouldn't return until late, so it was up to me to feed the hungry bunch. They practiced at the church on Thursday evening, but since they had added two songs to their performance, they needed the extra practice tonight.

When I get home after work, I'll put Momma to work baking her famous chocolate-frosted brownies, I thought, *the ones she made before she moved to Florida and got on the healthy eating wagon.* That would keep her busy and make her feel like an important part of preparing for the show. I don't know why, but I felt that was important.

AT SIX-THIRTY, the aroma of warm, just-baked brownies grabbed the attention of six noisy teenagers as they piled into the living room and immediately made themselves at home. Draped on the sofa, sprawled on the floor, tossing the oversized floor cushions back and forth and making jokes, the teens acted carefree and happy. My heart swelled with affection for each one of them. A bonus in the hunkalicious form of Joe Camps added a bouquet of happy thoughts blossoming inside my head.

"Are those brownies I smell?" Granville was the first to ask, but the others chimed in as soon as Momma walked into the room. Her face lit up like she'd won First Prize in a baking contest. I was glad I'd asked her to help.

"Yes, they're homemade, too. Not out of a boxed mix." I doubted that made any difference to this bunch of kids, but I knew it did to her.

"You'll have to wait until after practice is over. No singing with your mouths full, remember?" I tempered my remarks with a grin. They knew the rules.

Joe sauntered over, eyed the plate of brownies, and bowed to Momma. "Ma'am, you are as lovely a lady as I've met in a long time. I'll bet you have a whole shelf full of gold medals from all the baking contests you've won, haven't you?"

Lord love a duck, I couldn't shovel fast enough to keep from getting buried in the deep stuff Joe was spreading. Momma kept on smiling and acting coy as a young girl, and Joe kept spreading until Momma insisted he take an extra brownie as he headed out to the garage. Talk about smooth, hoowee! The man was an expert.

After I got the kids settled down to serious singing, I meandered out to see if Joe was making any headway with MinnieV. I know, I know. That wasn't my only reason to go out there, but it worked for me.

Joe had his head under the hood. I sidled up and took a look, too. "How's it going?"

"You need an oil change to begin with, but other than that, I haven't found the cause of the odd noise. You may have to take it to a repair shop where they can put it up on a hoist. Or where they have a computer they can hook it up to and get a read-out of the electric system. How old is your van, anyway?"

"Old enough to be needing major repairs, I'm afraid," I told him. "I'm not going in debt right now for that or anything else."

I took two folding lawn chairs from behind a stack of packing boxes. Joe took them from me, setting them side by side and holding one for me. I thanked him and sat. He pulled the other one closer and sat next to me.

"Guess what happened at the church today, when Gus and I dismantled the overflow drain in the baptistery?"

"What? Who paid for that, by the way? The church?"

Joe chuckled. "You sure ask a lot of questions, don't you? Sure you're not on the police squad? For your information, we were hired by your favorite people, the Ruby Springs Police Department. Detective Hardy asked Gus to clean it out, and you'll never guess what we found."

"I'm not good at guessing games, Joe. Just tell me in plain words. To heck with games."

"Of all the crazy things to find, a man's pink tie was caught in the trap. How the heck something like that got in there, Lord only knows. You should've seen Gus's face. I thought he'd never stop laughing. What man in his right mind would wear something like that?"

Joe kept talking, but my mind was jumping around like dice in a Yahtzee cup, trying to remember where I'd seen a tie like that. Pink! Pinkpinkpink . . . Of course! The photo at the mansion. The one with Poke, Parvis, and WILBUR HADLEY! Wilbur was wearing a pink tie with the summer seersucker suit like the one he wore to the deacons' meeting the night of the murder.

I wanted to call Detective Hardy right away and tell him what I suspected, but I'd have to wait until the kids and Joe were gone. I couldn't even confide in Joe. Not yet.

"Hey, Earth to Frankie Lou!" Joe reached over and took my hand. "Where'd you go? All of a sudden you were miles away."

A little sigh slipped from my lips. "Sorry, I was thinking about the kids' performance coming up. I'll admit I'm nervous. What if the crowd doesn't like them? They're darn good singers, but I remember how critical the community can be. Especially of kids who represent new traditions."

"You worry too much, Frankie Lou. You've done a great job with the kids, and they want to do their best and make you proud. Everything will be fine." He tipped my face up with one finger. "Stay cool. The kids have your back. And so do I."

I smiled up into Joe's face. It wasn't easy playing it cool when in truth I wasn't feeling cool at all. It had been a long, long time since a man had touched me.

Chapter Sixteen

Long after Joe left, The Joyful Noise kids went home, and Momma snored softly in the bedroom next to my sleeping daughter, I tossed and turned on the sofa, rehashing my phone conversation with Detective Hardy. I'd told him about the photo and Deacon Hadley's pink tie, but he'd blown off the possibility that it might lead him to the real suspect and suggested again that I leave the investigating to the police. Huh! Like they were moving forward on the case.

I flopped over on my stomach and shoved my head under my pillow. I heard a banging noise outside. Thinking Moses was rummaging for scraps in the garbage can, I got up, grabbed a broom out of the hall closet and ran out the front door to shoo him back home. Instead of a tomcat, I surprised a gnome-like figure wearing a ski mask coming out of the garage, his hand bloody from the broken window glass on the service door behind him.

Miss Nettie screeched, "Stop right there! I know it's you, Wilbur Hadley!" He started to run, with something tucked under his arm.

I chased after him down the driveway waving the broom. "Stop, or I'll call the cops!" I gave the broom a wild toss and smacked him in the back hard enough to make him stagger. He turned and made a mad dash away from my house, right into the double barrels of Miss Nettie's shotgun! Lord love a duck!

"Thought I heard a varmint out here," she called out to me. "Looks like you caught a big 'un, Frankie Lou. I got him cornered." My fearless neighbor stood there waving the no-nonsense weapon at the perspiring, ashen-faced Wilbur. "Stay where you are, Deacon. Mess with me and I'll blast you into next Sunday, and it won't be for church. I already called the cops, and they're on the way. Take that silly thing off your face before you smother."

I ran past the startled deacon and reached Miss Nettie. "Where on earth did you get that gun?" My heart was pounding, but she looked cool as a cucumber in her colorful Hawaiian muumuu and big ol' shotgun. She never ceased to amaze me.

"Your daddy didn't need it anymore once he and your momma moved to Florida," she said with a sly grin. "Now go get something to bind up Wilbur's hand so he'll quit bleeding like a stuck hog all over the sidewalk."

I ran back into the house for bandages, leaving Miss "Wild West" Nettie and her shotgun in charge of Wilbur. Despite the commotion, Momma and Betsy were still asleep. "Thank you Jesus," I whispered.

"MR. HADLEY, WHY did you break into my garage?" I asked, wrapping a clean towel around his bloody hand. "I don't own anything valuable."

He shook so hard I thought he might go into shock. He had several small cuts from the flying glass, but none that looked severe.

Wilbur looked to Miss Nettie, his sad eyes pleading for permission to speak. She nodded but kept the shotgun leveled at his chest.

"I'm so s-sorry, Frankie Lou," he said, his eyes filling with tears. "No one was supposed to get hurt! Everything I did was for her. For Poppy Rose," he sobbed. "Now it doesn't matter."

"But that doesn't make any sense, Mr. Hadley. What did you do for Poppy, and why doesn't it matter now?"

"When are the police coming?" he asked. "I need to see them. I have to confess. Yes, I must do that right away." He was perspiring so badly it was difficult to tell what was sweat and what was tears.

Miss Nettie shifted her shotgun lower. "Oh, you'll see 'em all right. Here they come." Wilbur moaned.

Sure enough, two cruisers and the detective's car sped toward us, lights flashing. They lined up in front of my house and Miss Nettie's and unloaded what looked like the entire Ruby Springs Police Department. Who was left to mind the station?

Detective Hardy strode up the sidewalk. "You can put away your gun now, Miss Nettie." He held out his hand for the weapon, but Miss Nettie shook her head.

"I'll just keep it handy until you boys find out what this man was doing in Frankie Lou's garage. He busted the glass out of the service door to get inside. Breaking and entering's a crime, you know."

"Yes ma'am, we know. We'll see that it's all taken care of."

"Well, see that you do," she snapped and rested the butt of the gun on the ground, like a soldier standing guard.

"You won't mind if I check your weapon to make sure it's unloaded, do you?" Detective Hardy asked. He took the 20-gauge shotgun before she could react. He broke it open and removed the shell from each barrel. "Where'd you get the gun, Miss Nettie? You've got enough ammo here to hunt bear. I'll help you lock the gun and these shells away. We don't want anyone getting hurt."

Miss Nettie stomped off into the garage in a huff, and I saw one of the policemen in there give a high sign to the others. They all moved out of her way.

CHIEF JACKSON had arrived with Detective Hardy and was in the process of questioning Mr. Hadley when he saw me talking to one of the officers and motioned me over. As soon as I walked up, Wilbur started babbling about being sorry and how he'd done it for Poppy, just as he'd told me. His apology still didn't make any sense.

"Mr. Hadley, please wait until the detective gets here so he can hear what you have to say. I promise you'll have a chance to tell us everything." The chief turned to me. "And Miz McMasters, I hope you can shed some light on this incident, too. Detective Hardy informed me of your earlier phone call—the one about a photo. But first, the detective and I have some questions for Mr. Hadley as soon as he finishes talking with your gun-totin' neighbor. I understand she's the one who reported the burglary."

"Yes, she did. She heard the noise when I did and came outside with her gun. I wouldn't have caught him without her help. I happen to have some questions of my own for Mr. Hadley, too."

"You'll have to wait while we hear him out, then you'll have your chance."

By the time the detective led Miss Nettie out of the garage after locking her shotgun and ammo away safely, Wilbur was so agitated he could hardly stand still. Cops with flashlights were swarming inside my garage like flies on a pile of cow pies. All we needed to complete the organized chaos was Momma adding her two cents worth into the mix. I prayed she wouldn't wake up until everyone was gone. I wanted my turn to ask Detective Hardy if the tie in the baptistery belonged to Wilbur and how it got there. And what had the crime lab found out from the blood samples they took from the dumpster? And why had Wilbur broken into my garage? Most of all, I wanted to look up and see Joe coming down the sidewalk toward me. What craziness had put that notion in my head?

Miss Nettie, bless her heart, sent two of the officers to her backyard for lawn chairs and ordered them set up in my driveway, so we could all sit down. Chief Jackson objected, but she soundly overruled him. Even unarmed she was full of gumption and grit.

"You don't expect us to stand around while you figure this mess out, do you Chief? Slow as this case has been moving, we'll be out here until next week."

Surprise of the day—the chief and everyone in uniform did as Miss Nettie said. Even portly Detective Hardy, who had trouble holding back a grin. I suspected he had an auntie or a grandma just like Miss Nettie.

What followed was the most unconventional burglary investigation in the history of Ruby Springs. And Momma was sleeping through it. *Hallelujah!*

Wilbur was so anxious to confess his crimes he gushed apologies to the chief and Detective Hardy at least six times in between his hard-to-believe explanations. The poor man became so excited he turned a pale shade of green and hyperventilated. Miss Nettie ran to her house for a paper bag so he could breathe into it until he calmed down. He looked like one of the living dead. I swear I thought we'd never get to hear the end of story.

Wilbur finally took his head out of the paper bag long enough to finish. "Poke deHaven sent Poppy Rose on a singles' cruise to find a rich husband and solve his financial woes. See, he loved women, and he loved gambling, but both vices were putting him close to bankruptcy."

Wilbur wiped his face with the hand that a medic had treated and re-bandaged, then gulped from a bottle of water. "Poke knew I worked for attorney Foster Gates and asked me to check financials in my company's files for marriageable candidates in the area around here. I told him about Parvis's stock portfolio, and he concocted a bogus contest so the unsuspecting millionaire held the winning ticket on a singles' cruise, then sent Poppy Rose on the same ship to snag him and bring him home to Daddy. Poke tried cozying up to his new son-in-law to get some insider help with investments, but Parvis wouldn't play along." Wilbur slumped back in his chair, gasping and exhausted from the trauma of confessing.

"A good slug of Mr. Daniels' finest will cure what ails ol' Wilbur," Miss Nettie told the chief. "Want me to fetch a shot for him? For medicinal purposes, of course."

Chief Jackson scowled. "You know better than that, Miss Nettie. I'll just pretend I didn't hear you."

"Well then, do something to keep the man talking, for goodness sakes!" Miss Nettie's attention span was shorter than a gnat's tonight, but this time I agreed with her.

"I still don't see what this has to do with Poppy's murder," I blurted out. As far as I could tell, I was still a suspect, and I wanted that resolved! "For cryin' out loud, who killed her?"

"Hush, child," Miss Nettie said, giving my arm a grandmotherly pat. "Wilbur's story is better than one of those TV crime shows. Let him talk." She slid a sideways glance at the chief. "Should I make popcorn?"

Wilbur let out a ghastly moan. Chief Jackson nearly slid off his folding chair. "No, Miss Nettie," he said gruffly. "No popcorn." A low rumble of laughter came from the policemen in the garage.

I grabbed another bottle of water for Wilbur from a cooler Miss Nettie had brought when she went home. For the second—or was it third?—time, the deacon revived enough to continue his tale, which got crazier by the minute with the revelation of his own part in skimming the Fremont books for Poke after Poppy cut her daddy off without a cent.

It was difficult to listen to the love-struck man relate how he tried to confess his thievery and his love for her to Poppy after the deacons' meeting the other night. Out in the parking lot, he'd tried to embrace her, but she spurned his advances, fighting him off and struggling. She hit her head against the dumpster when she fell.

"She wouldn't listen to me, so I dragged her inside the church. I had to use the tape to make her stop screaming. That was the only way she could hear me tell her I loved her." He sobbed through his words. "Dear God, that's when I realized she'd never hear anything I had to say. She was dead." Wilbur covered his face with his hands. His sobs were so loud now, if Momma heard the commotion, she'd come flying out of the house faster than a sneeze through a screen door. Fortunately, Detective Hardy allowed Wilbur a minute to get control of his emotions, but I kept an eye out for Momma, just in case.

The entire time I sat there listening to the deacon's confession, I kept remembering how Poppy Rose looked when I found her at the bottom of the baptistery. How could he say he loved her and still engage in such a dreadful act as murder? I knew it wasn't my turn to question the suspect but I'd waited long enough. I was growing gray hairs waiting for answers. "Mr. Hadley, if you loved Poppy Rose so much and knew she was dead, why'd you dump her in the baptistery?"

"I panicked when I saw blood on her head and clothing. I thought the water would wash away any evidence. When I saw you going to the church, I fled the scene and made the 9-1-1 call so the police would find you there."

Detective Hardy studied the remorseful Wilbur before he asked the question I'd been waiting to hear most. "Mr. Hadley, can you explain why you broke into Miz McMasters's garage?"

"Poke had gone to the Fremont home to retrieve the doctored files containing my figures and the Fremont bank accounts. He couldn't find the files and told me I'd better bring them to him by midnight or I'd be sorry. I was in the house to get them when Frankie Lou showed up, so I had to knock her out. I didn't know if she'd seen me or not, so I hid the files in a toolbox I'd seen upstairs and ran out of the house."

Wilbur stumbled through the rest of his tale, leaving us all aghast. He'd seen Joe and I leave with Gus's toolbox and knew it was in my garage. He waited until we went to bed and broke in to get the files out. The rest of his confession made his bizarre recitation easier to believe. Weird, but believable. Ruby Springs was in for a shock after the police released the truth.

Detective Hardy called out an all points on Poke and Delilah, adding a gruff apology to me before loading Wilbur into his car. It wasn't much, but it was enough. I had my life back, plus maybe a little more if Joe stuck around. *Thank you, Lord.*

THE GRAY, METAL folding chairs donated for the evening by Lindorf's Rent-or-Buy were all set up on the side lawn of the Faith Community Church, ready for the evening's festivities, thanks to Miss Nettie and Momma. The fact that the company's advertising was in bright yellow lettering on the back of every chair was part of the deal Miss Nettie made with Homer Lindorf. Momma had also finagled Flowers by Floralee to donate two large arrangements of assorted gladiolas and ferns, one for each side of the portable, wooden platform Joe and Gus had built especially for the fundraiser.

Earlier in the week, the kids had unanimously voted on Wesley as their spokesperson to give a little background speech about how The Joyful Noise originated. I'd encouraged them make their decision without any input from me. Playing favorites wasn't the way to promote harmony within the group. Besides, I wanted the townspeople to see exactly what these kids had to offer the community as productive future leaders. Tonight was their night to shine.

Wesley had protested at first, saying he wasn't any good at public speaking, but Bruno evidently did some serious convincing. Joy gave him a big hug and said she believed in him. That was all it took to make Wesley cave.

Tonight when he stepped in front of the mic at exactly seven o'clock, the audience—which was larger than I'd dared to hope for—quieted down to hear what he had to say. I didn't have a clue what kind of introduction he'd prepared. My only advice had been to simply talk naturally. He told me Joe had given him the same advice before they left home. If that was the case, Joe must be here tonight, but I hadn't seen him in the crowd before I sat down.

Wesley tapped the mic to make sure it was working, looked at me sitting in the front row and winked. He'd done the same thing several times while we were setting up. I wanted to holler, "You go, Wesley!" Instead, I smiled proudly and gave him a thumbs-up.

"Good evening, ladies and gentlemen," he began. His voice was steady and clear. "The Joyful Noise singers want to thank y'all for coming out tonight. We've got some foot-stompin', hand-clappin', make-you-happy music we hope you'll enjoy. We've been rehearsing real hard with Miz Frankie Lou's help. She's fought for us in a lot of ways y'all probably aren't aware of."

He paused to clear his throat. "You see, the six of us kids like to sing, and we think we're pretty good, but it was Miz Frankie Lou who showed us how to blend our voices and make a joyful noise. So that's exactly what we want to do tonight for y'all. We hope everyone here will be feelin' uplifted and joyful after you hear us sing, 'cause if you're happy, then we'll be happy, too."

Right on cue, the excited singers literally danced onto the stage ready to begin their first set of songs. All decked out in their favorite camo outfits, they smiled at the audience and took their places. Bruno riffed on his guitar, and Granville pounded out the intro on a second-hand portable keyboard.

My heart stood still waiting for the first song to begin. Had I forgotten anything? Would the kids remember the words?

"*This little light of mine* . . ." A jazzed up version of the first song I ever learned in Sunday School filled the evening air with happy voices. Joyful Noise? You betcha!

Beside me, Betsy tapped her foot and hummed along. She'd already hinted she wanted to join the group next year. Before long she'd be a teenager. Sooo not ready to deal with that milestone. I know all about the angst and drama those years can bring.

I sneaked a look at the people seated on either side of me and gave a sigh of relief. They weren't smiling, but they weren't frowning, either. I wanted to turn around and study the faces of those seated behind me, but that would've been too obvious. Instead, I sat there nervous as a five-year-old on the very first day of school.

The song ended, and I died at least three times in the long moment of silence that followed. One clap at a time the applause built in intensity until the entire audience was clapping.

The singers beamed and took a step forward to bow. Then Bruno strummed a few chords while he waited for the crowd to quiet down before starting the next song, *Waltz Across Texas*. Couldn't get more country than that. The kids did the old classic proud. They'd rock Summer Fest, no doubt.

Through the entire program, The Joyful Noise sang and danced their hearts out. The crowd applauded every song, giving the same enthusiastic approval to the group's mix of gospel, country, and pop tunes. Their final song of the evening, Louis Armstrong's classic *What a Wonderful World*, gained the loudest approval.

While the audience was still applauding the finale, Wesley walked to the mic and raised his hands for the crowd's attention.

"What's going on?" I asked and took a step toward the stage, but Wesley shook his head and waved me back to my seat. Okay, now I was reeeally nervous. We hadn't planned an encore. Then it hit me. He wanted to thank the people again. Relieved, I sat back, thinking what a thoughtful gesture from the group.

A low murmur ran through the crowd as heads turned toward the back of the gathering. I did the same. Oh, dear heart! Joe strode up the left side of the chairs and onto the stage. Stood right up there beside Wesley, for gosh sakes! What was he doing?

"Folks, this is my dad, Joe Camps. He and The Joyful Noise have planned a special surprise for our director." Wesley looked straight at me with one hand on his heart. "Miz Frankie Lou, we thank you for believing in us. For giving us hope and encouraging us to believe in ourselves. We chose this song to let you know we believe in you, too." He stepped aside and handed the mic to Joe.

Dead silence fell over the crowd for the second time tonight. Then Bruno played an introductory chord, and Joe started to sing.

Surprise didn't even begin to describe my feelings right then. It was a come-to-Jesus moment I would never forget as long as I lived. My instincts had been right all along. "My" kids, The Joyful Noise, were worth every minute I'd spent working with them. I was so darn proud of them, my heart overflowed with love. And Joe . . . well, I suspected all along he was one of the good guys. But what I hadn't realized until now was how he made me feel as a woman. I still couldn't wrap my mind around those feelings—didn't know quite what to do with them, so I settled on waiting until later to examine their meaning.

I listened with a full heart as Joe's rich baritone filled the soft, Texas twilight with words of hope and the promise of *Peace in the Valley*. *What a voice!*

What a man! But there was so much more to him than I knew. So much more I wanted to know. So much to . . . love?

Joe's eyes met mine, and in that sweet moment, all the anxieties of the past melted away. Someday, there will be peace in Ruby Springs, I believe that with all my heart. The future looks brighter for everyone now that The Joyful Noise—and Joe—are in our lives. Whatever the future holds, I can't wait for the next phase to begin. *Hallelujah, Amen!*

About The Author

Serving up her own batch of deep-fried sass by the page full, Lora Lee's first mystery *Bringing In The Thieves*, Book 1 of the *Joyful Noise Mysteries*, is set in the type of Southern small-town the author knows so well. Revolving around the world of choirs, glee clubs and the well-intentioned shenanigans of a close-knit church community (Bless their hearts!), the series stars single mom, Frankie Lou McMasters—a preacher's kid who fell from grace—and her misfit group of teenage singers who form The Joyful Noise. Mix in a body in the baptistery and a wrongfully-convicted ex-con with a golden voice, and it adds up to a heap of sour notes in Ruby Springs, Texas, with Frankie Lou fixin' to find out what's what before she gets the blame, like always.

Keep in tune with The Joyful Noise at JoyfulNoiseMysteries.com

Born in a small town in the Texas Hill Country, Lora Lee discovered the magic of reading at an early age and began inventing stories before she could write down the words. Her preacher daddy, as well as her mama, encouraged her love of books by making certain she always had a library card each time they moved to a new town. Known to her supportive critique group as LL or Tex, author Lora Lee is Mom to her four children and Grandma to her nine grandchildren and five great-grandchildren. With hubby by her side, she enjoys their exuberant family gatherings when all twenty-six members join them for good food and noisy ball games in the backyard.

Lora Lee also writes as Loralee Lillibridge. Learn more about her contemporary romances at Loraleelillibridge.blogspot.com and Loraleelillibridge.com

Lora Lee

Made in the USA
Lexington, KY
20 April 2019